D1460472

The Strawberry Harvest

Paul Wokes

Bright Pen

Visit us online at www.authorsonline.co.uk

A Bright Pen Book

Text Copyright © Paul Wokes 2013

Cover design by Katy Dynes ©

British Library Cataloguing Publication Data.
A catalogue record for this book is available from the British Library

ISBN: 978 - 0 7552-1562-1

Authors OnLine Ltd
19 The Cinques
Gamlingay, Sandy
Bedfordshire SG19 3NU
England

This book is also available in e-book format, details of which are available at www.authorsonline.co.uk

Thanks:

The author has received help from many people in writing this book:

Inspirational help has come from Dariusz Lesniewski, Ann Marie Kelly, Katy Dynes, Allan Marshall, Joanne Edwards, Theresa Jonsen and Ioana-Raluca Andreiu.

Technical support has been given by Emelia Jonsen, Matt Bennett and Richard and James Fitt.

Special thanks must go to my sister, Sylvia Wan, who has supported my efforts throughout the entire writing process and painstakingly edited the book.

Paul Wokes:

Paul was born in the county of Lincolnshire, England. A teacher by profession, he has inspired many pupils to strive to reach their highest potential. He has represented his county at bridge, chess and badminton and plays an active part in the life of the local community. His motto is: 'there are no limits!'

Part One:

Chapter One: The War years

I was born in Woodhall Spa in Lincolnshire, towards the end of the Second World War. My mother, bless her heart, was a wonderfully kind lady with a heart of gold. Unfortunately, she suffered from a nervous disposition and the German bombing raids over our small village gave her no chance to overcome this debilitating trait.

Woodhall Spa had a small airfield and there were others close by: East Kirkby, Coningsby, Waddington, Cranwell and Scopwick to mention but a few. The reason for so many airfields was simply that the flat land of the Fens provided ideal runways for our Spitfires and Lancasters. The German bombers knew this and were determined to put as many of them out of action as possible. As soon as one runway was repaired the Heinkels and Junkers would return to wreak more havoc. It was during one such raid that the centre of our village was ripped apart. This particular raid was remembered by war survivors many years after the conflict was over. A large bomb detonated in the centre the village, wiping out the Royal Hydro Hotel and Winter Gardens and many of the surrounding shops. I was never told how many people died in this raid, possibly my parents did not know, or maybe they did not want to recall the horrors of this dreadful time in their lives. But as a youngster I can vividly recall walking past this scene of utter destruction, as it was many years before the debris was carted away and new buildings replaced those shattered by war. If you visit this area today, you can see a memorial to the 617 'Dambuster' Squadron.

My grandfather was a train driver by profession and as we grew older and more curious about the war, he would entertain us with stories from his time in the war. One particular story always fascinated me, my brother and my two sisters and still does to this day. He explained that the 'blackouts' made it difficult for the

German pilots to find their targets, so any sign of light would act as a beacon to their navigators. The hot furnace of the steam trains was like a magnet attracting bees to a honey pot. The German planes would follow the train to its destination, believing that they would be guided unerringly to their target. The train drivers were fully aware of the situation and as soon as they detected hostile aircraft above the train they would deliberately head for the nearest side line, away from any town, village or airfield, and then run like the devil before the bombs started descending! Grandpa told us that he had taken such evasive action on more than one occasion!

Our father was excused military call up. His profession as a dispensing chemist was considered too vital to put his life at risk. However, he was part of the village fire-fighting force. This may sound a trivial task compared to those actively sacrificing their lives to prevent Hitler over-running our country, but it was more important than one might realise. Once Hitler gave up his attempt to destroy our airfields, he turned some of his attention to destroying our crops and where better to start than in Lincolnshire, with its fertile fields producing much needed grain for the war effort? The incendiary bombs were much smaller than those used to destroy airfields and buildings and the risks to the pilots were much less as by and large the flat Fen fields were not defended by Spitfires or anti-aircraft guns. So once the air-raid siren had sounded the 'all clear', the intrepid villagers with their tin hats and witches' brooms, rushed into the fields to beat out the fires, reminiscent of the actions of the Dad's Army platoon led by Captain Mainwaring!

As Goering's Luftwaffe continued to bomb our airfields and set fire to our crops, propaganda leaflets were dropped over much of the county to persuade us that our resistance to the German war effort was futile.

It was during my first year of teaching History at the William Lovell School in Stickney that one of the fourth year pupils brought into school an actual Nazi propaganda leaflet. He told me that his father had spotted this on the main A16 road running through Stickney and decided to keep it, rather than destroy it. Most of the villagers on spotting these leaflets had torn them up on the spot, or taken them home to burn on their fires, but for some inexplicable reason this gentleman had decided to retain his copy and now his son was asking me if I would like to keep it! I was delighted at the chance to possess such a vital piece of war memorabilia and offered to pay him something for the privilege of owning it. But the boy was adamant that his father would accept nothing in return for his gift. He deemed that giving his son an enthusiasm for the study of History was more than enough reward in his eyes.

To this day, I still possess the original document and have printed a copy of it on the following page. I make no apologies for this because I believe that it links me with the past, present and future. The importance of my father's fire fighting has been clarified and I have a much clearer understanding of the importance of my role as a teacher.

The Battle of the Atlantic is being lost!

The reasons why:

1. German U-boats, German bombers and the German fleet sink and seriously damage between them every month a total of 700 000 to 1 million tons of British and allied shipping.

2. All attempts at finding a satisfactory means of defence against the German U-boats or the German bombers have failed disastrously.

3. Even President Roosevelt has openly stated that for every five ships sunk by Germany, Britain and America between them can only build two new ones. All attempts to launch a larger shipbuilding programme in America have failed.

4. Britain is no longer in a position to secure her avenues of supply. The population of Britain has to do with about half the ration that the population of Germany gets. Britain, herself, can only support 40 % of her population from her own resources in spite of the attempts made to increase the amount of land under cultivation. If the war is continued until 1942, 60 % of the population of Britain will starve!

All this means that starvation in Britain is not to be staved off. At the most it can be postponed, but whether starvation comes this year or at the beginning of next doesn't make a ha'porth of difference. Britain must starve because she is being cut off from her supplies.

Britain's losing the Battle of the Atlantic means Britain's losing the war!

Chapter Two: Primary & Junior Schools

War with all its horrors was the back-drop to my entry into this world and as far back as my memory can recall I suffered from the debilitating effects of asthma and eczema. In my childhood years, there were no Ventalin sprays to expand the airways during attacks and the resultant struggle to breathe caused a slight curvature of my upper spine and a rounding of my shoulders. Despite these setbacks I was determined to lead as normal a life as possible and not allow the asthma to restrict my activities.

Asthma attacks occurred every three to four weeks and usually lasted for about three days: on day one I sat for most of the day and night on the edge of my bed struggling to breathe; by day two I became exhausted from lack of sleep and finally fell into a fitful slumber; this relaxed me and by day three I was on the mend; day four saw me back to full health!

When I was not suffering from an asthma attack I was otherwise fit and healthy! But once I reached the age of five, my school attendance was blighted by this unfortunate illness and I missed a lot of vital schooling.

Casting my mind back into this formative time of my life, I can remember little of my early school days. The one clear memory I have retained, has nothing to do with my academic progress and everything to do with my social life in the play ground! At about the age of six, I can distinctly recall one particular play time when the Blueberry twins were running a game of 'catch' and I asked them if I could join in. They were pretty young girls and I really did want to be part of their game. For some reason unbeknown to me, they refused to allow me to join in and I was mortified. Children can be so cruel at times and I have never forgotten this feeling of rejection! In my own teaching career I have always looked out for the unpopular underdog, the misfit who is never invited to join in the communal games. I have a soft spot for such children and try to protect them from these kind of cruelties in their developing years.

Our Primary School building was a large former house and apart from the playground disappointment with the Blueberry twins, I spent a happy few years at this school before transferring to the Junior School much closer to where we lived. The Woodhall Spa Junior School was very small with no more than sixty pupils attending. These were the immediate post war years and the male population had been decimated, resulting in fewer children. In fact the shortage of male labour was so bad that the government authorised many Italians and Poles to live and work in England so that the rebuilding programme could start in earnest. Many former prisoners of war and many foreigners who had fought for us in the war were employed in the same way. It is estimated that over 300,000 immigrants were working in post war England.

As I had now reached the ripe old age of seven, my memory and understanding were developing apace. Food and clothes rationing was still in force and everyone had to exist on the bare minimum; there were no luxuries. However, as a vegetarian, my father was allowed to trade his meat and fish coupons for extra rations of sugar, cheese and butter. Sugar sandwiches were one of our rare Sunday treats!

Another event that caused great excitement in our family was when my grandfather was driving the steam train past the end of our garden. Once a week, he would be scheduled on the Horncastle to Kirkstead route, a side-line which passed through Woodhall Spa before joining the main lines to the large towns of Lincoln and Peterborough. As he drove past our back garden he would tell the fireman to slow the train right down so he could stand on the foot plate and gently throw out a parcel wrapped in brown paper and tied with string. We waved to grandfather as the train re-gathered its speed, collected the parcel and rushed indoors to open it. How our grandfather managed to obtain such a quantity of rare treats was beyond our comprehension and it never ceased to amaze me how generous he and grandma were! They must have been saving their rations all week to purchase the jam, marmalade, biscuits and sweets that were all contained in these heavenly packages from the gods!

At school I excelled at Maths but was not so hot in English. I was a reasonable reader for my age, but a terrible writer. My lack of ability in the written language was not helped by my enforced absences to recover from the recurring asthma attacks.

As at the Primary school, my most memorable achievement at the Junior School was not an academic one. During most of my lessons Peter Burgess chose to sit next to me. I did not particularly like the boy because he was not the least interested in improving his academic skills, preferring instead to try and distract me from my studies. He would frequently nudge my elbow as I was writing, resulting in my hieroglyphics becoming even more illegible than usual! I mentioned this continual nuisance to my parents and they spoke to the form teacher. As a result of this we were separated in class. This was a great relief to me and my studies gained a greater momentum, but far from my troubles being over, at breaks and lunchtimes he would take every opportunity to harass me in whatever way he saw fit. His favourite trick occurred after school when I was keen to cycle home to greet my brother and sisters. He would grab my bike and refuse to hand it back; standing in an insolent, threatening manner, he would shout out:

'What are you going to do about it, Shelby?'

After several days of this torment, my temper finally broke and I told him I was going to fight him.

A crowd of several children gathered around, anticipating an interesting encounter; Peter was renowned as a school bully and few had ever dared cross his path.

The fight was an anti-climax; he threw a few punches and I responded with a few. Not many of these reached their intended facial target and those that did lacked sufficient force to do any real damage, so the fight ended in a whimper. However, the mere fact that I stood up to him seemed to have a far reaching effect upon Peter Burgess and he handed my bike back without a murmur. From this point on I was his best 'buddy' and suffered no further abuse from him; in fact he became my loyal protector and quickly offered his assistance should anyone else dare to threaten me!

Much later I learned from my parents that my form teacher had witnessed the entire fracas and decided not to intervene as he believed the fight would probably solve the issues of unrest between Peter Burgess and me. His judgement proved to be right!

At eleven years of age all pupils had to take their eleven plus, a selection exam to see if they could gain sufficient marks to obtain a place at Horncastle Grammar School. My sister Sylvia had already secured her place two years earlier and so now the pressure was on me to do likewise.

Unfortunately, on the day of the tests I had an attack of asthma. Determined not to be denied a place by default, I forced myself to attend the Saturday morning test, but I was certainly not at my mental best by any means. I also suffered from another distinct disadvantage of which I was unaware at that time. At the Woodhall Spa Junior School the staff had given no formal training to the aspiring candidates on how to complete the tasks which were set. These mostly comprised I.Q. puzzles, which I personally found absolutely fascinating. No one gave me any tactical training: no one suggested that it would be a good plan to complete all the easy questions as quickly as possible then turn to the more difficult ones. So I spent the entire time meticulously solving every puzzle, in sequence, no matter how difficult it was or how long it took!

When the supervising teacher told us to put our pens down, I had only completed a small section of the allotted tasks! No wonder I failed to obtain a place at the Grammar School! I did learn later that I had not failed the test abysmally; I was in fact a borderline candidate. The Headmaster, Jim Belton, had to make the final decision and he erred on the side of caution believing that my frequent asthma attacks would put enormous pressure on my academic progress and cause me untold stress and strain at the Grammar School, whereas I would be well suited to the slower academic pace of a secondary modern school. His prognosis was probably correct and by such small decisions my future course was set!

Chapter Three: Boarding School

The sense of failure at not passing my 'eleven plus' exam was somewhat dissipated by my parents' decision to move to Letchworth in Hertfordshire. As a youngster I could not understand the reasons behind this huge venture and now, looking back from my advanced years, I am none the wiser why our parents even considered allowing the family to face the disruption to our lives that such an operation would entail. The move would require my father to sell his pharmaceutical business, to find work as a chemist in an alien town, to locate suitable affordable accommodation in Letchworth and a complete change of schools for all four children. I must admit that I was inwardly less than enthusiastic about the whole idea. But despite her nervous disposition, my mother was a powerful figure when it came to carrying out her wishes and she had made up her mind that a move to Letchworth was what we all needed!

One of the main motivating forces for such a move was probably the allure of a vegetarian boarding school in Letchworth, called St Christopher's. The plan was that the two oldest children, Sylvia and I, would lead the vanguard of the Shelbys' migration to this new city. We would both be enrolled as boarders at the school until my father could sell his business and the whole family could be re-united. As a plan it was well thought out and organised, but who would have realised that selling his business would prove an impossible task for Arthur Shelby! There were no takers at the right price, if indeed any at all!

Meanwhile, in September 1954, Sylvia and I started at our new school. The school grounds were massive and there were many buildings scattered around their site. As Sylvia was three years older than me she was placed in a different House, in a different part of the school and I rarely saw her from one day to the next.

This was the first time that I had ever been away from home

and not being around my brother and sisters hit me hard. I was very lonely and became depressed. The school discipline seemed to veer from one extreme to the other. At supper time, some pupils would become very boisterous and totally out of control. The general behaviour would vary according to which teacher was in charge of proceedings, but I was mortified when on some occasions bread, jam and margarine were thrown across the table, with total disregard or respect for their intrinsic value. This was a far cry from my memories of austerity immediately after the war when food was a precious commodity to be valued, cherished and shared.

If discipline at some meal times was non-existent, in the morning it was over-bearing. Every morning throughout the year, regardless of the weather, the day would start with a cold shower followed by a one mile run! This routine was designed to strengthen us mentally and physically, but I detested it and the cold water invariably caused me breathing problems. Mostly, I struggled through the daily ordeal without protest but one day my asthma was particularly severe and I informed the teacher that I was too unwell to take a cold shower or run the statutory mile. Did I receive any concession for my illness? No! In fact the teacher tried to force me to take the cold shower. Although very wheezy and short of breath, my adrenal glands were working overtime and I swung and punched at the teacher until he relented and told me to go to the dormitory and lie down.

By midday I felt slightly better and asked to see my sister Sylvia, but my request was turned down by the House Master and his decision was subsequently backed by the Head Master, after appeal by me to this higher authority. This was the final straw! I felt like a prisoner in a concentration camp, not like a pupil in a supposedly forward-looking enlightened school. I took out my writing pad and swiftly penned a short letter to my parents. In it, I described my current poor state of health, the refusal of the Head Master to allow me to see Sylvia and the over-all depression I felt most days. I referred to the Head as 'a pig' and I threatened that if my parents did not travel to Letchworth to take me away from this horrendous situation, I would start hitch-hiking home on Saturday morning! Meanwhile Sylvia was enjoying the life at boarding school and had no idea of the storm that was brewing!

Saturday dawned bright but cold, with a thin watery sun and few clouds. I had already packed my meagre belongings, when at midday I was summoned to the Head Master's office in the main school building. My irate mother and father had arrived and informed the Head in no uncertain terms that they were withdrawing both Sylvia and me from the school with immediate effect. The Head tried in his syrupy best voice to persuade my parents to change their mind. I'm sure he was more concerned over the loss of revenue than the loss of two of his star pupils! But his efforts met with a steely determination from both my parents not to back down. He asked the reasons for our withdrawal and my mother cited his refusal to allow me to see my sister as the crucial one. 'What kind of establishment are you running here anyway?' she asked in an accusing tone of voice. 'A concentration camp?'

Nice one mother! I thought. Give him both barrels!

As though reading my mind, she did not disappoint my inward desires.

'Let me read to you the letter we received from our son a few days ago.'

I must admit that although I dashed off the letter very quickly it was well crafted and showed the school in a very uncaring, almost negligent light, especially in the way they had ignored my serious asthma attack.

The Head's jaw dropped. 'I'm sure this was all a terrible misunderstanding, a lack of communication between members of staff and something that we can soon address.'

His words fell on stony ground; my mother continued to read aloud the contents of the letter. When she reached the sentence where I had described the Head Master as 'a pig' his face contorted with fury. He realised that nothing he could say would change the situation and he stomped out of the office to instruct his secretary to summon Sylvia.

Our Letchworth venture was truly over and I was delighted to leave behind the school which had blighted three months of my life. Looking back at the experience and trying to find something positive about it, I can only recall one aspect of boarding school life that benefitted me in the future. Keith, one of the more friendly pupils in my House, had offered to teach me how to play chess and spent many patient hours in the dormitory, teaching me the delights of this wonderful game. By the time I left this school I was a half decent chess player! Despite this one small redeeming part of the whole experience, I promised myself that if I ever had any children of my own I would never send them to boarding school!

Chapter Four: Secondary School

Now that the Letchworth venture was well and truly aborted, my parents had to arrange schools for both Sylvia and I to attend. In Sylvia's case this was fairly straightforward: she returned to Horncastle Grammar and struggled to catch up on the work she had missed. In my case the situation was not quite as clear-cut. I had failed the eleven plus exam and was not entitled to a place at the Grammar School. My options were somewhat limited! After some consideration, my parents decided to send me to Gartree Secondary Modern. This school had only been open for a few months; in fact it was opened in September 1954, the month of my ill-fated admission to St. Christopher's Boarding School in Letchworth.

The school was situated in the small village of Tattershall, renowned locally for its famous castle built by Ralph Cromwell. It was approximately four miles from Woodhall Spa and free bus transport was provided by the County Council.

I was so relieved to be far away from the horrors of St Christopher's and amongst children that I felt akin to, that I soon settled into the daily school routine. The school was well-run and well-disciplined and because I was happy I made good progress in all subjects. My over-all memories of this school are very positive ones.

At this time in the UK's history, attending local cinemas to watch films was relatively expensive, but Gartee School started its own film club and I joined a group of four children from my village who became members of this club. We biked to the school to watch free films. I loved the sense of freedom and adventure that this after-school activity generated in me. I was finally maturing as a young adult and my asthma attacks were becoming less frequent.

The Shelby family were all vegetarians by conviction - in fact my paternal grandfather had founded the Liverpool Vegetarian Society. At school, I tried my best to keep this part of my life a secret. Few people understood vegetarians and we were considered to be rather oddball and cranky in our ideals. If my fellow pupils had known about my quirky diet they would have tormented me mercilessly - a situation I was keen to avoid at all costs. So my mother prepared sandwiches for me and arranged for me to eat these at a friend's shop, just down the road from the school. This worked extremely well for me. Everyone at the school assumed I was going home for lunch and no questions were ever asked.

During the first few years at Gartee, I never questioned my parents' vegetarian ideology; I went along with it like all dutiful children do, accepting my parent's beliefs and customs until I became old enough to start to think about them for myself. Then once my questioning mind 'kicked in' and I started to ponder on the whole ethos of this distinct way of life, I was not sure that I agreed with my parents or wanted to follow this difficult, non-conformist journey. Clarification of how I felt about the whole issue came to me suddenly and abruptly one hot afternoon when my form was engaged in a lesson of Rural Studies.

This was one of my favourite subjects because in decent weather we had the chance to go outdoors and plant, tend and harvest different vegetables. The school owned about half an acre of garden and this enabled the senior classes to take responsibility for cultivating their own plots. As many of the school pupils came from farming backgrounds, their ability in this subject was apparent for all to see: neat rows of lettuces, radishes, potatoes and many other flourishing vegetables. Although I enjoyed this lesson I had little practical experience of growing crops and opted to assist one of my friends with his allotment rather than have my own. We agreed to split the results of our labour.

As the sun scorched down on our group of hard-working young farmers, one boy spotted a bat hanging upside down on the wire netting which separated the school's land from the neighbouring farmer's land. All sixteen boys curiously gathered around the sleeping mammal. Then one of the boys used his garden fork to knock the innocent creature off the wire and it fell to the ground. How I wished the bat would open its wings and fly away to safety! No such miracle, life-saving response happened. It was still in a comatose state from its daily sleep and barely responded to the rude awakening.

Stung into action, I shouted out: 'Leave the bat alone! What harm has it done to you?' I rushed at the boy whose fork was suspended in mid-air ready to strike the poor defenceless animal. I succeeded in knocking him sideways away from the bat, but soon other boys joined him and started to push and jostle me. I was tearful but at the same time hysterical with fury. Despite my frantic efforts to save the bat's life, I was powerless to prevent the needless act of cruelty which followed. Three boys restrained me whilst several boys started to use their forks to spear the tiny creature as it struggled to take off. It was writhing in pain as the blows rained down. Finally its life was snuffed out and I was released. My emotions were shattered and I felt a keen sense of failure: I had not been able to save the bat's life.

However, the whole tragic incident did have some positive end product – I finally realised that I was a whole-hearted believer in the vegetarian way of life; a humanitarian way of life which extolled the worth of every living creature and which believed that human beings did not need to kill animals for food in order to survive; nor should they kill animals for the gratuitous thrill of the power of life over death!

Chapter Five: Horncastle Grammar School

Although I had failed to pass the initial selection exam for entry to the Grammar School, I did have a second chance a year later when I re-took the test, but once again I was turned down! It was now that my parents showed their total belief in me by paying for private tuition in Latin . They reasoned that at some time in the future I would be given a chance to attend the Grammar School and that when that time came I would need a language to gain a place in University. What foresight, imagination and commitment they showed! No one could wish for more dedicated parents than I had.

I attended Gartree Secondary Modern School long before ROSLA was passed by the government. ROSLA (the Raising of School Leaving Age) was the acronym for the Act of Parliament, which changed the age at which pupils could legally leave school. From 1962 onwards, pupils had to remain at school until they were sixteen, but prior to this act of parliament, pupils, at secondary modern schools like Gartree, had to leave at the end of the fourth year when they were only fifteen years of age and with no academic qualifications whatsoever.

Fortunately, at the end of my fourth year I was given a 'free' transfer to Horncastle Grammar School. This time, thank goodness, there was no exam involved! But the downside of this arrangement was that I had to repeat my fourth year; this was decreed necessary to allow me to have two years of preparation for my 'O' level exams as opposed to the one year if I had entered year five. As it turned out it was not a bad thing because it gave me another year to adjust to the higher academic standards expected from pupils at this selective school.

I loved the rarefied atmosphere of this mixed secondary school. I was in my own element, where pupils strove to be the best. Success was viewed as desirable object not as something to be kept secret for fear of derision and reprisals.

My 'O' level results were satisfactory; the grades ranged from a 'D' in Technical Drawing to a 'B' in History and Geography. Suffice it to say they were sufficiently high to allow me to sign on for 'A' levels in History, Geography and English Literature.

If my 'O' level grades were satisfactory, my 'A' level grades were outstanding! I was awarded subject prizes in Geography and History for obtaining the best grades of all the pupils taking these subjects. It was now that I began to understand the phrase 'late developer' which had often been used to describe me!

Not only were my academic standards of the highest level, I also started to excel at football and cricket. The school under 18 football team was one of the best in the county and I was selected to play at right back. Playing in mid-field was my friend, Alec Bradley. He had signed junior contract forms with Grimsby Town and was regularly picked to play in their first team, in Division Two of the Football Associations League. Other players in our team were as equally skilled as Alec but possibly less ambitious about attending trials at top League clubs. Our goalie was the eighth wonder of the world: he had lost complete sight in his left eye and his eyeball had been replaced by a glass orb, but despite this enormous handicap he made some heroic saves and frequently spared my blushes when a speedy left winger had avoided my desperate sliding tackle!

Chess provided another social outlet for my energy and drive. The tuition I had received at St Christopher's School finally paid off: not only did I play on board two of the Grammar School Team, but I was also asked to play for Horncastle Town Chess Team. This team played in division one of the Lincolnshire League and we travelled to distant places like Scunthorpe, Grimsby, Grantham and Lincoln to pit our wits against some very experienced players.

Many adults extol the virtue of our school days and tell us to make sure that we enjoy them to the full. I certainly carried out these instructions and every day for me was full of new experiences and I was contented and happy.

Chapter Six: Hull University

My 'A' level results were sufficiently impressive to obtain the offer of a place to study Honours Geography at more than one university. Why did I choose Hull? Because the Professor who interviewed me at Hull was by far the most friendly of all those I encountered. I did not choose my university on grounds of its academic brilliance; I simply went for the one with the friendliest faculty!

My three years at the university passed like a cloud on a summery day. No sooner had I undergone my Fresher's Day than I was collecting my degree from the University Dean.

Of course, the period in between these two events was full of action: at the end of my first year I switched from studying Geography and History to studying Theology. The main reason for the change was not really an academic one but a philosophical one. Studying Geography and History did not fulfil my idea of what universities were all about. I wanted to be part of a revolutionary learning process where student and lecturers would engage in fierce debate and move the boundaries of human knowledge forward to new heights! I suppose this viewpoint was too simplistic and naive, but it was what I expected and what I needed to keep me motivated. To be honest, I found the Geography course rather dull and boring.

Some time before the Easter vacation, I mentioned my feelings to a fellow Geography student and he suggested that I should apply to join the Philosophical Faculty as he felt that this subject would fulfil more of my ideals. I took his advice and was disappointed to learn that this department already had its full quota of students for the forthcoming year. So in desperation, I applied to join the Theology Department and was welcomed with open arms. This change of direction meant that I had to stay at university for a further year and this year would not be funded by a government grant, but I was certain that I could earn sufficient money in the generously long vacations so that the financial burden would not fall too heavily on my parents.

The social side of university was brilliant. I learnt how to play Bridge; firstly by watching a group of four Mathematical students play the game and later by asking all kinds of curious, silly questions about what was going on! Occasionally when one of the four was missing, I would be invited to step in as a replacement.

As an experienced chess player my skills were highly sought after and I soon secured a place in the university 'A' team, playing in division one of the Yorkshire League. The standard of play in this division was much higher than the standard I had encountered in Lincolnshire; but all the team members were real chess enthusiasts and we frequently attended practice sessions where we passed on our individual areas of expertise to the other members of the team. We also spent a considerable amount of time studying opening and defensive tactics.

My chess achievements culminated during Rag Week in the final year of my studies when with another member of the chess club I was invited to attempt to break the world record for playing continuous chess. I certainly had heard of the Guiness Book of (World) Records and I had even seen Norris and Ross McWhirter on television supervising world record attempts in various events, but, strange though it may seem, I was not aware of any world records in the sphere of chess. All that changed when I was introduced to Bernie. Although he was an enthusiastic member of the chess club, he didn't play in either of the two university teams, so I had only seen him occasionally and knew little about him.

One evening at the club, he engineered an opportunity to challenge me to a game. I instantly realised that playing a competitive game of chess was far from his mind, so we quickly agreed a 'draw' and made our way to the refectory where he insisted on buying me a cup of coffee. Over our coffees, the discussion became very animated. He asked me if I was interested in trying to break the world chess record for playing continuous chess. He

21

told me that he had attempted this on his own the previous year and given up after 50 hours. He felt that two people would have a much greater chance of succeeding than one.

To this day I am not sure why he honoured me with the chance to be his chosen partner, but I am eternally grateful for this wonderful opportunity to excel at the highest level. Having one failed attempt under his belt, Bernie had organised this year's effort meticulously. He had persuaded a clothing shop in the centre of the town to allow us to place a table and chairs in their bay window from where we could attempt to beat the previous world record of 65 hours. A restaurant a few doors away had agreed to supply us with food and drink.

When he finally asked me if I wanted to join him I did not even think about my answer. 'Yes!' I responded with great enthusiasm. 'I would love to have a go!'

To me the situation was a 'no-brainer'! Bernie had done all the donkey work organising the event, why would I not want to take part?

We decided that our world attempt would take place during the first few days of Rag Week, as this would give us a chance to recover mentally and physically before the onset of our final exams. Two days before we were due to start, Bernie dropped his bombshell.

'I've decided not to go ahead, because I don't really think I can manage any more than the fifty hours I completed last year. But you can still have a go on your own. During the daytime you can play members of the public and at night I have organised a rota of chess club members to carry out two hour shifts, so that you will never be without an opponent.'

It took a while for me to assess the new dimension to the situation. It would not be so easy for me to motivate myself when I didn't have a constant companion to keep me going. My overwhelming emotion was one of disappointment that Bernie would not be able to share in my triumph if I managed to succeed; after all, it was his brainchild and his organisational skills that were making my effort possible. However, after weighing up all the imponderables, I decided to go ahead with the challenge.

The decision as to when to start the world attempt was left in my own hands. I reasoned that the best time would be early in the morning after a good night's sleep. The logic was flawless, but the good night's sleep eluded me! I slept fitfully for what seemed like a few hours before rising at 7.00am to eat a light breakfast of egg on toast and drink a cup of coffee.

From the outskirts of Kingston–upon–Hull where I lodged with Nancy, a very pleasant landlady who treated me like her son, I drove to the multi-storey car park in the centre of town. The Council had very kindly agreed to wave all parking charges during my world attempt, so I didn't have to worry about a huge fee when I finally left their building.

I officially began my record attempt at 9.15 on the 24th June 1965. Many of my memories of the event have faded with the passage of time, but some aspects remain crystal clear. Throughout the day time I had many challenges from Naval College students whose campus was close by. They had to pay a fee to challenge me and if they won they received a free copy of the university Rag Week magazine. During the first day I did not lose any games, nor did I lose any during the morning of day two, but as the afternoon of day two dragged on I found it increasingly difficult to concentrate and started to lose rather regularly! Fortunately, I had an endless supply of Rag Week magazines to hand out to the winners and the money from challengers kept rolling in!

Some wise soul had told me that the most difficult time to stay awake was the period around 3.00am to 4.00am. This I found to be true and on the second night it became a constant struggle to stay awake. I had to exercise extreme will power to prevent myself from falling asleep at the table. My eyes would frequently close for a few brief seconds, but a well delivered kick under the table would instantly arouse me! As the first flush of dawn lightened the sky, my energy levels would rise and my spirits would soar.

In 1965 there were no organised ten minute breaks every hour. I was allowed short toilet breaks, but otherwise I was always playing chess. I even ate my meals and drank my gallons of coffee at the table where I was playing chess. Bernie was a star! He popped along many times during the day to encourage me and make sure there were always opponents for me to play and during the night, he took the longest most unpopular shifts. Without him, I would never have succeeded.

Finally at 2.15am on 27th June 1965 I passed the previous world marathon record. I was both exhausted and elated at the same time. I continued to play on until 5.15am, smashing the previous record by three hours. The dawning of the third day brought a new lease of energy and I felt capable of continuing for several more hours, but common sense prevailed and on account of my forthcoming Finals, I decided it was time to quit! The local newspaper, the Yorkshire Post, had followed my record attempt throughout the three days and one of their reporters was there at 5.15am to shake my hand and take my photo. Although feeling dog-tired, I appreciated this gesture of support.

I drove back to my lodgings and Nancy was there waiting to greet me at the door. She was over the moon with excitement; she warmly congratulated me and then gave me a huge, lasting hug. When she asked me how I felt, I told her that I was OK but really tired and desperately needed a hot bath to revive my energy. She told me she would prepare a light breakfast whilst I enjoyed my bath.

After giving my body a quick scrub and washing my hair, I felt like a new man. But suddenly a wave of utter exhaustion overtook me and I felt that I was falling asleep in the bath. With a supreme effort I climbed out of the bath and without even drying myself rushed into my bedroom and crashed out naked on my bed. It was fifteen hours before I awoke from my deep slumber!

Little more remains to be said about the actual record, other than in December 1965 I received a complimentary copy of the Guiness Book of Records with my world record printed under the heading of Chess Marathon. I could now officially claim that I was a world record holder!

Despite the large amount of time I devoted to chess and bridge, I set myself the target of studying for at least forty hours each week. The average working week at this time was forty hours and I felt that it was only fair to complete a comparable amount of weekly study. Furthermore, I knew my parents were making a huge financial sacrifice in order for their children to attend university.

Some of the women on the course went way above my target hours, only to suffer from stress and strain and then they failed to complete all their final exams. Fortunately, I did not fall into this trap and studied conscientiously but not to the extent of damaging my health.

At the end of my three years of study I obtained a second class Honours Degree in Theology with ancillary History of which I am very proud.

Chapter Seven: Teacher Training College

In my last year at Hull University I considered training as a P.E. teacher but ruled this out because of the asthma. I fleetingly thought of training as a minister for the Church of England and even considered the idea of taking over my father's pharmacy business, but finally drifted into a teaching career after a fellow student had suggested that teaching was not such a bad option on account of the long holidays!

Rather than complete my post graduate teaching course at Hull, I decided to travel to Goldsmiths' College in London where my sister Sylvia had carried out her teacher training two years previously.

Apart from a minor hitch at the start when I had a bad attack of asthma, the first term went smoothly enough. In the second term I had to complete a ten week teaching practice. The school allocated for this was Kingsdale Comprehensive in the East End of London. This provided a real introduction into the downside of teaching. I observed one lesson where a teacher from Australia failed miserably to control a class of thirty-two, rowdy third year pupils. At no point in the lesson did Mr Peterson gain any semblance of control. He shouted instructions at the top of his voice to try and overcome the noise coming from the majority of pupils, whilst Bibles were thrown across the class, some covers tearing off in the process. What was so sad about the nightmare scenario was the small number of pupils sitting quietly on the front row who were trying to listen and learn.

I had my own problems, mostly with 7PT. I never learnt what the 'PT' stood for; suffice to say that this was one of the lowest ability classes in the entire year seven. There were only fifteen boys in the class, mostly black, all of them possessed with an irrepressible desire to move around the classroom at will. Despite my most strenuous efforts, after about five minutes or so several pupils would alight from their chairs and start to wander around the classroom. I tried cajoling them, praising them, bribing them with merits, threatening them with dire punishments, all to no avail; they persisted in jumping off their chairs and joining their friends who were sitting at different tables. In desperation, I turned to the Head of the Religious Education Department for advice. Mr Jones suggested that I should come and watch him teach this particular class. I willingly agreed and the next day found my way to the back of room seventeen where I seated myself on a small chair, behind one of the pupil's desks.

On the stroke of 10.00am Mr Jones marched briskly into the room followed by the fifteen pupils of 7PT. So far, so good! The class started in an orderly fashion and brief, straightforward instructions were given to the pupils as to their tasks for the lesson. After five minutes had elapsed, almost as though on cue, one of the boys in the front row climbed off his chair and started to wander towards his friend's desk in the second row. Mr Jones raised himself to his full six feet height, puffed out his chest and roared: 'Did I tell you to move, boy?'

The boy remained silent.

'Come out here!'

Taking a five foot length of bamboo cane which was conveniently leaning against the bookcase, he swished this through the air several times as the pupil apprehensively approached.

'Hold out your hand, boy!'

The pupil timidly complied. Swish! The cane descended at considerable speed onto the boy's hand. He yelped and pulled back his smarting hand.

'Go and sit down boy and don't leave your seat again unless I tell you to!'

Throughout the remainder of the lesson no one left their seats!

Enlightenment dawned on me. So this was how to control 7PT - with fear and intimidation! As a student teacher, I wasn't allowed to use the cane even if I wanted to, and in truth I had no heart to wield this frightening weapon. So peace and harmony were not a feature of 7PT's remaining lessons on my teaching practise in Kingsdale Comprehensive!

However, teaching the other classes went remarkably well and for the most part lessons were orderly and productive. There were incidents. I remember well the occasion when a lad called Sylvan Stoner took out a knife with a six inch blade and repeatedly started to stab the desk top with it. I made a rapid assessment of the situation. Looking Sylvan in the eyes, I summoned my most powerful commanding voice:

'Stoner, put that knife away in the desk!'

The class all turned round to see what would happen. Stoner stared back at me, measuring his response. Slowly and deliberately he opened the desk top and slid the knife into the dark cavity.

The lesson concluded without further incident and I duly reported what had happened to Mr Jones.

'Leave it with me Paul! I'll take a colleague and sort it out.'

Asked later by Mr Jones what I would have done if Stoner had not put the knife away I was non-committal.

'Well I certainly wouldn't have marched down the classroom to Stoner's desk and tried to take the knife off him!'

On another occasion, the bell rang and I was about to release my favourite year seven class for their mid-morning break when I heard raucous sounds coming from the corridor outside the room where I was teaching. Cautiously peering out of the door I saw a scene of utter chaos. It was as though a gigantic rugby scrum was taking place; about one hundred pupils were pushing in one direction and about the same number were pushing in the opposite direction. At one end of the scrum was the Headmaster, blowing his whistle and shouting at pupils to stop their pushing and stand still, at the other end was the Deputy Head issuing the same instructions. No one took any notice. The only way to clear the gridlock was to peel the pupils off one at a time and send them away from the fracas. It took about fifteen minutes to clear the logjam. By this time break was nearly over but at least I could now let my pupils leave the room safely.

Had I believed that all teaching was as difficult as that at

Kingsdale, I would have ended my teaching career there and then. In fact my sister Delphine, endured only one day of her teaching practice at a London school before tendering her resignation. Attempting to teach maths to a class of predominantly black girls she was sworn at by one of the pupils, who added,

'You're not going to tell me what to do, you white trash!'

Having been told by her head of department that she would have to get used to this sort of banter from the pupils, she informed him in no uncertain terms that this was not the case and immediately left to embark on an engineering career at De Havilland Aircraft Company!

I was optimistic that teaching in some sleepy, rural village in Lincolnshire would be far different from the experiences of teaching in an inner city comprehensive. I was certain the pupils would be more polite and keen to learn, so I successfully completed my allotted ten week stint in the East End of London.

Chapter Eight:
The William Lovell Secondary School

Having obtained my Post Graduate Teaching Certificate, I was now in a position to apply to Lincolnshire County Council for a teaching post. Rather than apply to individual schools as teachers have to do today, at this time the Council informed me of all schools in the area where I wanted to work that had vacancies in History, Geography or Religious Education. I soon discovered that R.E. teachers were in short supply in Lincolnshire and was told of several schools with vacancies in this subject. History and Geography were more popular choices for teachers and there was less availability. In all, I attended three interviews: one at a Grammar school, one at a Comprehensive school and one at a Secondary Modern. Two of these interviews were for R.E. and one was for History. I was successful in all my interviews and offered all three posts. I suppose this wealth of offers was very flattering, but my choice was very straightforward. When I attended the interview at the William Lovell School in Stickney I bumped into a familiar figure in the corridor on my way out of the Head's office: Alec Bradley, my friend from Horncastle Grammar!

Since leaving the Grammar School I had lost touch with Alec and assumed that he was pursuing a football career with Grimsby Town. Obviously I was wrong. His parents had persuaded him that even if he succeeded as a player and was offered a full time contract, his career would be a very short one. Furthermore any serious injury could end his contract prematurely. They insisted that he should gain some qualifications in another area, so he would not be totally reliant on football for a living. Alec had followed their advice and was now head of P.E. at the William Lovell School.

He took me into the staff room and made me a cup of coffee. We caught up on the main events of the missing years and then started on the serious business of assessing the school. Alec told me that it was a wonderful school with pleasant, polite, hard-working pupils. He thoroughly recommended that I should join him as a member of staff at the school as head of History. This I did. It was a decision I never regretted!

During my teaching career at the William Lovell School I served under a total of five different Heads. I suppose this must prove something! Either I was very resilient, or the Heads suffered from a fast 'burn out' rate. Probably a bit of both!

Each Head was different and each had their own styles of management. In the early years of my teaching career there were no Ofsted inspections and teachers were left to get on with their own job with very little interference from either the County Council or the senior teachers at the school.

In my first year, I was classed as a Probationary Teacher and could only progress to a professional teacher if my first year's teaching was judged to be satisfactory. I am not sure how the decision to accept me as a competent teacher was reached, because during my first year no members of the school staff watched any of my lessons and the inspector from the County Council briefly popped in to watch half an hour of one lesson. Hardly time to make a detailed assessment of my ability! But pass I did and my career as a teacher was under way.

I suppose most teachers would be able to recall some details from their first year of teaching. One or two of my memories are crystal clear. I was teaching a fourth year class of about twenty-five pupils. We were reading a History text book about the First World War. In the book it described the major naval battle off the coast of Jutland. The author stated that Britain won the battle and as a result of this the German fleet rarely ventured forth again.

One of the pupils sitting in the front row shot his hand into the air.

'Yes, Barry?' I said.

'Please sir, that is not correct!'

Taken aback by this assertion, I asked rather meekly: 'And how do you know that Barry?'

'Because I love naval history and have studied the First and Second World Wars in detail. At the Battle of Jutland, the British and German losses were about equal - if anything, slightly fewer German ships were sunk than British ships.'

Amazed at Barry's detailed knowledge of such events, I requested that next lesson he should bring in evidence to verify his claim. This is exactly what he did and the whole class spent a fascinating lesson studying Barry's naval books and making up their own minds as to what really happened in the battle. I introduced the issue of bias in writing and when the bell went at the end of the lesson no one wanted to leave!

It was not just one student in this class that caught my attention; it was several of them. One might think that secondary modern pupils who had failed their eleven plus exam would not be as academically bright as those pupils chosen to attend the Grammar and High schools, but this was just not the case with this class. Many of the class would compare favourably with the pupils from the Grammar and High School. I knew the William Lovell School students certainly had the determination to succeed, but they would sometimes ironically remind me that they were 'failures' so I should not expect too much of them!

The chess exploits of six pupils from this particular class are legendary and have been recorded in the annals of the school's history. After some intense lunch-time and after-school training, I entered them in the Sunday Times Schools' Chess Championship.

The early rounds were against local schools and having defeated them all, the team were drawn against opponents from further afield, like Grimsby, Scunthorpe and Lincoln. Their progress against teams from such large towns and cities was nothing short of phenomenal and having been victorious against all the Lincolnshire Schools, they were invited to represent Lincolnshire in the East Midlands' final. This was a real honour and was living proof that 'failed' pupils could compete successfully against anyone in the country.

Their winning streak ended when they narrowly lost to

Wiggeston Grammar School, by three and a half points to two and a half. My disappointment was equally matched by my elation at reaching so far in the competition and more importantly, seeing the new sense of belief that these six pupils displayed.

I was curious to know how these pupils would progress once they had left the William Lovell School. Two of them stayed in the local area where it was easy to keep track of them. I heard little of the other four until twenty years later when Allan, a former member of the chess team, organised a school re-union!

This is how they had fared: Barry had gained his private pilot's licence but decided not to fly for the RAF, opting instead to work in I.T. Currently, he is working in Technical Sales for a private company providing software for the police; Chris trained to be a teacher and was now working as a Deputy Head at a Lincolnshire School not far away from the William Lovell; David owned his own garage; Andrew was working as a Loss Adjuster for an insurance company; Richard had won the National Pairs Bowling Championship and was the Sales Manager of an Indoor Bowls Company and Allan was making shed-loads of money working for an America company selling accident insurance and in his spare time playing chess for the county team!

I have often engaged in discussions about how the current teaching methods compare with those in the past. I try to be honest in my analysis. I agree that today pupils are given a chance to study a much wider curriculum and there is no doubt that computers have improved the presentation of pupil's work. But is the standard of work they achieve today any higher than in the past? I somehow doubt it! I do not believe that those six pupils from the William Lovell chess team would have reached any greater heights by studying in the modern education system.

Chapter Nine: Village Life

My first few years teaching at the William Lovell School were idyllic. As I had surmised when facing the rigours of teaching in the East End of London, the classroom discipline in the quiet, rural areas of Lincolnshire was so different from that of my teaching practice. There were no knife incidents; nor corridor scrums and most of the pupils conducted themselves in an orderly fashion and were keen to learn. Yes there were minor incidents, but nothing that couldn't be handled quickly and easily.

Fast forward ten years and there was a worrying trend in the growth of drug-related incidents. Rumours circulated that drugs had become a major issue in many of the inner city schools. Now these problems were beginning to emerge in the farmland areas of Lincolnshire, mostly because many families were moving out of the London conurbation and purchasing property in cheaper residential counties like Lincolnshire and Norfolk.

Some of these families settled quickly to the slower pace of the countryside and their children brought a new dimension to the classroom, but others did not fit into their new environment so well. Their offspring brought in the less desirable habits of their former life style, including the smoking of cannabis, glue sniffing and occasionally snorting cocaine.

I always made my classes line up in an orderly fashion outside my class door before allowing them into the room. On one occasion, as I watched the third year class file in, I noticed that Stephen Smith's eyes had a glazed look about them. I made a mental note to keep a watchful eye out for any trouble from him. Sure enough, Stephen seemed very agitated and was constantly distracting James who was sitting next to him. I decided to take pre-emptory action: walking over to where Stephen was sitting I ordered him to move and sit at the teacher's table. This was one of my favourite techniques for dealing with disruptive pupils, as it had the effect of isolating them from their fellow companions but at the same time ensuring that they were right under my nose if they started to re-offend. Mind you, this didn't work with all pupils; the 'smart arse' who loved to show off to the class would cause mayhem at the teacher's desk by pulling faces and making rude gestures whenever I was not watching him. But this morning, Stephen was very surly and unlikely to play the fool to the class. I stood behind and slightly to the side of Stephen's desk as I gave my command. Stephen, feigning obedience, rose slowly to his feet then, with a sudden change of pace, swung his fist at me. It missed my chin by a whisker, as I moved away equally as swiftly as Stephen had risen. Some sixth sense had warned me that Stephen was not going to act reasonably. As Stephen's extended arm shot past my face, I grabbed it and used the momentum to force him face downwards onto the classroom floor. Kneeling on his back so that Stephen's face was pressed hard onto the cold, tiled floor I spoke firmly to him.

'Stephen, if I let you get up, I trust that you will not take another swing at me and that you will go to my table and get on with your work.'

There was no reply from the prostrate figure on the floor. Slowly I eased my knee away from Stephen's back and allowed him to rise. I was mentally preparing myself for another physical assault, but what happened next took me totally by surprise. Stephen rose slowly and groggily to his feet and started to walk towards my desk. As I relaxed and heaved an inward sigh of relief, Stephen suddenly turned sideways and like a startled jack rabbit shot for the classroom door. Before I could react, Stephen had opened the door and was running pell-mell across the lawn and out of the school gates.

The pupils were stunned into silence. Finally, Jane said: 'Aren't you going after him, Sir?'

Of all the actions that went through my head, chasing after a fit year nine pupil with a hundred metre start was not one of them!

'No!' I replied. 'I'm sure he will come back when he's ready!'

At the end of the lesson, I informed the Head Mistress of Stephen's actions and duly filled out a yellow incident form.

Stephen was missing all of the next week and I had almost forgotten about the altercation when on the following Friday I was summoned to the Head Mistress's office. I was surprised to learn that the Head wanted me to visit Stephen's grandparents who lived in the village of Carrington about two miles away. Apparently, when Stephen exited my classroom at speed he had run all of the two miles to his grandparents' house where he was living.

The grandparents were having major problems with Stephen and had requested advice and help from the school. The Head suggested that I would be the best person to speak to the grandparents as I knew Stephen better than anyone else in the school and had experience of Social Work. However, it was left entirely up to me whether to undertake this parental liaison or not. Because I enjoyed a challenge I enthusiastically accepted the commission.

Having lived in the village of Stickney for over ten years I knew where the village of Carrington was situated but was not certain where the Smiths' house was. As it turned out, the grandparents' house was easy to find as all the inhabitants of Carrington knew the names and location of everyone living in the village. So when I leant out of my car window to ask an elderly, grey-haired pedestrian, where the Smiths lived I was instantly pointed in the right direction.

Almost as soon as I stopped my brown-coloured Mini on the wide gravelled drive I saw an elderly lady walking towards me. *The Head must have informed Stephen's grandparents of my arrival time*, I thought, *because she had obviously been watching for me from the kitchen window.*

As she approached, I guessed from her youthful complexion she was a lot younger than I had first surmised. Her slightly stooped appearance belied her real age. The problems associated with bringing up a troublesome teenager, like Stephen, had put years on her! She suggested that we sit outside on a garden seat rather than enter the house where Stephen was. It was a beautiful day in May and this seemed like an excellent idea, as it was an isolated location where we could not be overheard or interrupted.

As we talked my heart went out to this kind, gentle lady who was trying her best to help her grandson and was having this kindness thrown back in her face. She was most concerned about Stephen's behaviour. Apparently, Stephen's mother and father had separated when he was eleven years old and neither of them wanted to look after him. In a fit of generosity, she and her husband had agreed to take on the responsibility. The first two years had proved demanding but they had coped. Now Stephen was associating with older children who were in trouble with the police. Her husband had found Stephen in their garage, sniffing glue. His behaviour had become very erratic and they could no longer control him. After the incident at school, he had refused to return there and was spending his time at home sniffing glue and wrecking the furniture, recently smashing the television and damaging the table and chairs. He was obviously out of control and I informed her that she and her husband should not have to put up with this behaviour. I suggested that she call the Social Services and have Stephen removed from their house and put into care.

The Grandma thanked me for this advice and said she would reluctantly contact Social Services. Stephen did not return to the school and I surmised that he had been placed into a care home in Boston.

Five years later I was staggered to read the headlines of the local Standard newspaper, *'Stephen Smith sentenced to eleven years in prison.'* According to the Standard reporter's account of events, Stephen had become a local drug dealer and when one of his customers had failed to come up with the money he owed, Stephen had blasted him with a sawn-off shot gun. Whether he had tried to kill him or merely put 'the frighteners' on him was not clear, but after the shot was fired the client lost most of his right arm and narrowly avoided death from loss of blood.

I thanked my lucky stars that Stephen did not seem to harbour a sense of revenge for his classroom humiliation and had not come looking for me with his sawn-off shot gun! The times they were a-changing: no longer was the countryside such a quiet, idyllic place!

Chapter Ten: Jane Gray

It was about this time that I moved from teaching only History and P.E. to teaching some R.E. as well. This was at the request of the Head Master as the main R.E. teacher had suddenly decided to take early retirement and her actions had left school in the lurch; so until a full time replacement could be appointed, I dropped some of my History lessons and supplemented them with R.E.

In the September of that year, along with the new intake, Jane Gray arrived. Not that I took any immediate notice of her. Looking back, I can remember little, at that time, that was exceptional about her, apart from her excellent performance at Sports Day and her bold conduct at the First Year Parents' Meeting.

It was always difficult at first year parents' evenings to think of something positive to say about all of the pupils, as we had only taught them for a limited amount of time. In Jane's case the problem was solved when she marched up to my desk with her mother in tow and declared: 'I've made a good start in R.E., haven't I, Mr Shelby?'

The question did not seem to demand an answer, so I merely nodded and with this gesture of approval Jane triumphantly led her Mum off to see the next subject teacher on her list. I thought to myself, *what a precocious child!* But inwardly wished all parental interviews were as brief and easy as this one!

It was in year nine that I was forced to take note of Jane. Year nine was an important year for the pupils of the William Lovell School as by the end of the summer term they had to choose their optional subjects for the start of their GCSE courses in September. Maths, English and Science were compulsory but four other subjects had to be chosen from the options' lists. In theory, the pupils could choose which four subjects they wanted, but in practice some subjects were more popular than others and rapidly became over-subscribed, so the teachers did have the final say in which pupils to accept for their subject.

Jane had the distinction of scoring zero marks in the R.E. test at the end of the Summer Term, so I was amazed to see her name on the options' list for R.E. I vividly remembered her sitting bolt upright at the back of the class and not attempting one single question on the paper. She had neatly written her name at the top of the A4 sheet of paper but ten minutes later had added nothing more! Everyone else in the room was busily scribbling answers to the questions but Jane's pen remained stationary on the desk top. Feeling slightly puzzled as to why Jane was making no effort to answer even the easiest of questions, I silently walked up to the side of her desk and whispered very quietly that she should be able to answer some of the questions because they were based on general knowledge and not on factual information, but Jane remained motionless and her pen stayed untouched on the desk top!

So why did she want to join the R.E. group for GCSE? Before I made any decision on whether to allow her to include this subject in her options, I decided to interview her and find out the reasons behind her choice. Jane seemed to have no clear reason for wanting to study R.E., other than the fact that she enjoyed the subject. I pointed out that although enjoying a subject was very important it should not be the main criteria for selecting an option and that her disastrous mark in the end of term test suggested that she had better options available! Jane was determined to join the R.E. set and could not be dissuaded. However, I had the final say and refused to allow her to take this subject.

The William Lovell School by national standards was a small, co-ed secondary school, with a total of only two hundred and fifty pupils. This small size meant the teachers knew all of the pupils very well and any concerns about pupils would be discussed at staff briefings held each morning between 8.25am and 8.45am. Towards the end of the Summer Term the name of Jane Gray was mentioned on more than one occasion. Her form teacher Mrs Wilson was concerned that Jane was falling behind with her coursework in several subjects and she had heard other pupils in the form saying that Jane was living in a house with a boyfriend, unsupervised by any adults. She had questioned Jane about this but had been assured that this was not the case and that her mother was staying with her. But, despite Jane's reassurances, Mrs Wilson remained very worried about the whole situation and wondered if the Social Services should be called in. The Head promised to carry out further investigations into the situation. I could not remember any resolution of this matter, but had other on-going interests, such as badminton, football and chess, to fully occupy my thoughts.

September saw the start of Jane's final year at school. She had caught up with the missing course work and her name didn't crop up in the staff briefings. When I was on playground duty I could not help noticing that she had matured into a very good looking fifth year. Her features were very similar to those of Bridget Bardot, sex icon of the fifties: small nose, light brown hair, cute rounded face with startling green-grey eyes. I felt a very strong physical attraction to her but was unwilling to transgress the boundary between teacher and pupil, so I consoled myself with the thought that I was far too busy to start dreaming of dating immature school girls, even if they were very attractive.

I had always been keen on sport and as soon as I had settled into the school routine of preparing lessons and marking the pupils' work, I started a badminton club. It was on a Friday evening after the lessons had finished. This was open to both male and female pupils and was always very well supported; in fact so much so that I had to restrict the number of pupils attending as there was only room for one badminton court in the gymnasium. As a result of my coaching the school boasted two very successful under sixteen teams, a girls' and a boys' team. It crossed my mind that Jane might make a half decent badminton player as she was a very good athlete and a skilled netball and tennis player, but she never showed any interest in joining the club, possibly still smarting from my refusal to allow her to join the R.E. group for GCSE!

At the end of June, the fifth year pupils left and the teachers gained a few extra free periods, technically these were for marking and preparation, but it was the year eleven work that generated the most marking and with the departure of these pupils, teachers could concentrate on preparing for the following academic year. These preparations included reviewing the year's teaching, changing any aspects of the syllabus that had not been successfully presented, making an audit of text books and exercise books, ordering new stock and many other aspects of the day-to-day running of a department. Because the William School catered for a very small number of pupils, most of the twenty-two teachers were in charge of their own departments although they didn't receive any remuneration for this.

I enjoyed the Summer Term, the extra free periods, the fine weather and the imminent six weeks' holidays. This year however, I had to admit that I felt a little sad that I was not going to see Jane Gray again.

Chapter Eleven: Involvement in the Village

During my early years teaching at the school I became heavily involved in the local village life. Four ex-pupils from the school decided to form a village football team and asked me if I was willing to help with the organisational side of this. I was only too willing to help out with the venture.

We entered a team in the local Sunday League. Preparations for our league debut were frantic. With only two weeks to go until the deadline for league entry we had nowhere to play, nor any kit to play in! However, both problems were solved very rapidly. A local farmer agreed to hire us his field for a nominal sum and the money to purchase shirts and socks for all the players came from the generosity of the local villagers, when the players made a door-to-door collection. They were staggered by the response. Not only did they have enough cash to purchase a full kit but there was enough left over to buy goal posts and nets!

The most challenging aspect of our home matches was the pre-match, pitch-clearing exercise which the players had to carry out before kick-off. The farmer had a small herd of beef cattle in the field which were being fattened for market. The field was large and being shy animals the steers posed no problems to the players, supporters, or match officials. However, they did generate a considerable amount of 'cow pats'! It was the responsibility of the home team to make sure their pitch was in a fit state for play, hence the pre-match, pitch-clearing exercise. On occasions, the odd cow pat would be missed and any opposition player falling foul of it would swear that it was a deliberate ploy to gain a home advantage!

The Stickney team playing in the Sunday League performed well and gained promotion from the lowest division in its first season. I played in defence and acquitted myself well becoming a very popular player with the numerous supporters who turned out for home matches. Several of the older female school pupils would turn up to support their village team and there was more than one who cast an admiring glance towards me but of Jane there was no sign!

The football team was now an established part of the village and the team virtually ran itself. My duties were minimal and I decided it was time to gauge the interest of the villagers in forming a badminton club. The School ran an Adult Education Programme and they agreed to advertise the badminton coaching in their forthcoming prospectus. The ten classes were to be on a Tuesday evening between 7.00pm and 9.00pm. In order for the classes to be economically viable there needed to be at least ten fee-paying adults who wanted to join.

On the induction evening I was eagerly waiting in the gymnasium to see how many people would turn up for the new course; hopefully at least twelve. I was bitterly disappointed when only two men arrived. Only one of these was wearing some semblance of the required clothing for badminton. The class would not be viable, but as I had been told I would be paid for the induction evening even if the course did not go ahead, I decided to use the two hours to give some basic training.

The time passed extremely quickly as I demonstrated overhead clears, drop shots, smashes and the basic rules of the game. Ken and Andy seemed to have quite an aptitude for the sport and practised the techniques with a great deal of enthusiasm and no little degree of skill. When the two hours were over, I explained to Ken and Andy that the course would not be going ahead as there were insufficient numbers to make it financially viable.

Ken was the first to speak. 'Oh no, Mr Shelby, don't worry! There are at least another ten people who want to join.'

I was taken aback! 'So where are they all?'

'They'll be here next week,' said Andy.

'So why didn't they come this week?'

'They wanted to make sure that the classes really were for beginners,' said Andy and Ken in unison. 'They didn't want to get embarrassed by a lot of experienced players.'

Ken explained that he and Andy had been sent along to 'suss

out' the situation. Now they could report back to the others that it really was for beginners and the rest would join.

This was not the first time I was amazed by the timidity of the villagers nor was it to be the last. I remembered one of my friends at University saying that the people of Lincolnshire took a long time to accept newcomers to their villages but once you became accepted they would be loyal friends for life. Sure enough, on the second Tuesday of the course ten further students arrived; six men and four ladies. Badminton in Stickney was on its way to becoming a regular feature of the village life.

After two years of Adult Education classes, the twelve members had learnt the basics of the game and could play men's, ladies' and mixed doubles to a reasonable standard. They were all very competitive on court and as they needed further challenges to maintain their motivation, we decided it was time to form a club and enter teams in the local leagues.

The school gymnasium wasn't ideal for playing matches as the roof was very low and beams hung down from the ceiling, stretching across the court and restricting the height for clearing the shuttle. But it was not expensive to hire the gymnasium because as a teacher at the school I was allowed a concessionary rate. I did check out the possibility of hiring a court in the nearby town but these courts were very expensive and mostly fully booked. The school hall it had to be!

The newly formed committee decided that for their first season they would enter one men's team and one mixed team. The men's team would play in division three of the Boston Men's League and the mixed team in division five of the South Lincolnshire Mixed League. These were the lowest leagues available in the area and the committee hoped that the players would have a chance to taste competitive badminton without being totally out of their depth.

When reviewing the first season's performance, I noted both teams had obtained much better results in their home matches than in their away ones. This was mainly due to the advantage of our low, fifteen foot ceiling. Stickney's players had developed the skill of hitting the shuttle between two protruding beams which caused the opposition to temporarily lose sight of the speeding 'bird' and often resulted in a miss-hit and an easy point. Away from home, the players' lack of experience resulted in many sound thrashings!

One particular match came to mind! We had played a men's match at Spalding - a long established club who owned their own premises and used feathered shuttlecocks for their matches as opposed to the much cheaper nylon shuttles with which Stickney played. Timing the feathered shuttlecocks proved a nightmare for the Stickney players and throughout the entire match there were few rallies at all. Frequently, the first swish of the racquet through the air was rapidly followed by a second swish as the players totally missed the shuttle on the first attempt and made a desperate lunge to try and connect with it on the second attempt before it hit the ground. On one occasion, Andy made his customary two swipes and missed but actually managed to connect with it on his third attempt and amazingly the shuttle went over the net! It was not a particularly good shot but the opposition were in such fits of laughter that they had given up on the rally and ended by applauding Andy's never-say-die attitude. It was embarrassing when the entire match was over in just under one hour! This was a humiliating experience and no pairs had scored more than five points in any one game. The players still had a lot of learning to undergo!

Despite these occasional setbacks, the players were totally committed to league badminton and vowed to learn from their mistakes and improve their standard for the following season. Within three years Stickney Badminton Club was flourishing. They had gained several new members and were now running four teams: two mixed, one men's and one ladies'.

The future seemed rosy for the club but dark storm clouds were unexpectedly looming. The financing of the school's premises was abruptly taken out of the hands of the school's Head and handed over to the County Council Education Committee. Immediately, the hourly price for hiring the hall doubled. This put a severe strain on the finances of the badminton club, each member having to pay a lot more money. To make matters worse, the hourly rate became even higher after midnight. As many of Stickney's matches were now very closely contested affairs, they often went past the midnight deadline and the club was seriously at risk of going financially bankrupt. An emergency meeting was called at the local pub (The Rose and Crown) to discuss the situation. It was well attended and all of those present expressed their determination to keep the club running. We brainstormed ideas for remedying the situation. The most sensible ones came under two headings: reduction of costs and looking for an alternative venue. Under the first category it was suggested that the club might be able to reach a private deal with the caretaker Sid Coultan who locked up after the matches. He was the only one who knew how long the matches went on for. Several members thought that a letter to the County Council appealing for a reduction of their charges might also yield some results. I promised to pursue both of these suggestions.

The letter of appeal to the County Council produced no reduction in fees. An impersonal reply was received, stating that the Council had decided to standardise their charges throughout the county and that the new fees represented excellent value for money. I had little faith in bureaucrats and was not surprised that the club's appeal had fallen on deaf ears. Nor was my effort to find an alternative venue any more successful. So the Badminton club's fate rested in the hands of the caretaker.

Sid, the school caretaker, was a kindly man through and through. He had lived in the village all of his life and was very supportive of all the activities that went on. In his earlier years, he had played football for a local village team in Stickford and had even attended a trial with Boston United, one of the top clubs in the south of the county. Regrettably, his footballing career had come to a premature end when he fractured the ligaments around the knee cap in his left leg. Despite this horrendous accident he joined the badminton club and became a keen and competitive member, even being selected to play in one of the local leagues.

When I approached him to discuss a deal for saving money on the hall, he was one hundred percent behind the club.

'Book the hall until 11.30pm!' he said, 'then let me know what time the match will really finish and I'll pop over and lock up. I only live across the road from the school, so it won't be a problem!'

'What a great fellow!' I thought. 'Wouldn't it be fantastic if all people were as helpful as Sid?'

The new deal with Sid provided a temporary solution to the club's financial problems, but in the long term I knew that the club needed to find a new venue.

Chapter Twelve: Fundraising

In September, the Stickney Parish Council invited a member of the Badminton Club to attend their next meeting as they were considering building a village hall. The population of Stickney, like so many of the surrounding villages, was rapidly increasing and the Parish Councillors felt it was time that the village amenities should be improved. A small building already existed. It was used by the Youth Club, the Table Tennis club and for the occasional bingo session, but it was of limited use for any other activity as it was only twelve feet high and had very little floor space.

There was plenty of poor quality agricultural land surrounding the Youth Club building and the Council felt that a new Village Hall should be constructed on this behind the present building. Possibly, the two buildings could be linked by a corridor and a joint committee could run both buildings? All potential users were invited to the meeting at the William Lovell School to ascertain the likely demand for such a development. I attended, representing the Badminton Club. I was amazed to see so many people at the meeting. In fact the school library was so crammed with bodies that several people who arrived just before the meeting was due to start had to stand at the back of the room.

After officially opening the meeting and thanking everybody for their attendance, the Chairman suggested that they should change the order of the Agenda to deal with the proposed new Village Hall first. In that way, those who were attending specifically for this item could leave once these discussions were over. Everybody nodded their approval and the discussions got under way.

I was surprised that most of the Youth Club Committee was against the idea of a new hall being built. They seemed prejudiced against the scheme from the start, as though the new building would take away their power and control of the present facilities.

One after another, they rose to their feet and voiced objections: *the new hall would not be used; no one would be willing to go on the committee; it would lie empty for most of the time and become vandalised by the local youth and the Parish Rates would have to be increased to pay for the building.* I was in despair. It seemed that the idea for a new hall was doomed to failure from the start, without both sides of the argument being presented.

Fortunately, Youth Club Committee members represented only a small percentage of those present and the remainder of the assembly seemed totally positive about the new scheme. Alec Bradley, my teaching colleague and the Youth Club leader, extolled the virtues of having a facility capable of staging badminton and five-a-side football matches. A representative from the Bowls Club said that they would form an Indoor Club and use the facility in winter when their outdoor ground was out of action. I finally managed to attract the eye of the Chairman and told the meeting that the newly formed Badminton Club would definitely be interested in using such a facility. Eventually after everyone had been given a chance to air their views a vote was taken. The result was an overwhelming endorsement for those in favour of the new development.

The Parish Council generously offered to fund half the cost of constructing the hall; the other half had to come from the villagers themselves. It was suggested that all parties interested in using the facility should immediately start to raise money for the project as the Council Officer explained that their offer of funding would only be available for three years.

I was not sure how the members of the Badminton Club would take to the idea of raising money for this new venture but I needn't have worried. They were very enthusiastic and totally innovative in their ideas. Paul Gosling, a local farmer, suggested that a clay pigeon shoot, with good cash prizes, would raise over £1,000. He was authorised to go ahead with this event and several members offered to help with the organising and the publicity.

The ladies decided to hold a summer fete with one main attraction and many side-stalls. I had some experience of running disco dances and I promised to organise a series of dances at the school, provided enough members would volunteer to help supervise on the evening of the event.

By December, the fundraising was well under way. Paul's clay pigeon shoot had exceeded all expectations and raised nearly £2,000. The first of the disco dances had been held at the school in October and had raised the sum of just over £400, the second one was scheduled for mid-November.

November arrived and the weather took a turn for the worse; the mild, dry October gave way to a cold, dreary spell. Whilst many people complained about the cold snap, it certainly did not detract from the numbers attending the second disco dance.

The gymnasium was packed with bodies and the licensed bar did a roaring trade. There was a good attendance from badminton members and we circulated as much as possible to keep a watchful eye out for any potential trouble. It was important that anyone who started to act aggressively should receive an immediate warning that eviction would swiftly follow. Apart from the support of the badminton members, the committee had decided to employ two bouncers from the Boston Karate Club. These men were worth their weight in gold! At the first sign of fighting the bouncers would immediately lift the offenders clean into the air and remove them from the hall, without their feet touching the ground!

The first dance had been held on a Saturday evening. This meant that due to the Sunday trading laws the bar must stop serving drinks at eleven thirty and the dance must finish at midnight. This second dance was on a Friday evening but the committee had decided that it should still finish at the same time as the previous one, as there was always a fair bit of clearing up afterwards and by midnight most of the helpers were exhausted and ready to retire home for a good night's sleep.

I did one last patrol around the gymnasium and my heart skipped a beat. Was I mistaken or was that Jane Gray dancing in the centre of the room? I hadn't seen her arrive at the dance, but that wasn't surprising considering how many people had poured in at around 8.00pm when the dance had started. Did she have a boyfriend? Certainly, a stocky well-developed youth seemed to be in close attendance, but whether he was with her or trying to 'crack on' to her it was impossible to judge. My intense interest was broken by Paul [clay pigeon fund-raiser] reminding me that we needed to announce the last dance and then get prepared for the clearing up.

The DJ thanked everyone for their support, announced the date of the next dance in December and put on, 'Take the last dance with me', a nice slow number which gave couples a chance to enjoy a final dance. I resisted the temptation to seek out Jane and ask her for the last dance. How embarrassing it would be if she turned me down and the badminton players witnessed my rejection!

The last number finished and there was a mass exodus of people heading for the main school doors towards the car park and their journey home. I paid the bouncers, thanked them for their help and then turned to the task of clearing up. Sid had arrived and took charge of operations. He informed the helpers that there was no need to sweep up the litter, comprising mostly of cigarette and crisp packets, because he was paid to do that and would see to it in the morning; the most important help the badminton players could give was to carry the tables and chairs back to the dining room where they would be needed for the pupils' lunch at midday on Monday.

I was fully engrossed in this task when I noticed that Jane was standing in the school entrance hall with a very agitated lady, whom I recognised as her mother. Mrs Gray was accosting anyone who would listen to her, asking for suggestions to solve her problem.

As I walked from the dining room back towards the gymnasium, Mrs Gray turned towards me imploringly and said, 'What can I do? My car has broken down on the outskirts of the village. A friendly motorist stopped and helped me to push it on to the grass verge clear of the main road but there is no garage open at this time of night and I am supposed to be taking Alice back to Boston with Jane.'

Although I consider myself to be a friendly person and would help anyone in distress, I was reluctant to get involved on this occasion as I was running the Lincolnshire School's Chess Tournament the next day and desperately needed a good night's sleep. But the thought that by helping out I might get closer to Jane far outweighed any concerns over my possible mental fatigue.

'OK,' I said, 'I'll see what I can come up with; in the meantime, get Alice and Jane to help with the moving of tables and chairs.'

With the added assistance of Alice and Jane, the dining room soon had its full complement of furniture and I could give my undivided attention to solving the problem of transportation to Boston. Almost instantly, the answer popped into my head.

'Mrs Gray, are you a good, safe driver?' I asked. 'Have you had any accidents recently?'

Mrs Gray was taken aback and slightly indignant.

'Well, I like to think that I am a good driver, and *no* I haven't had any accidents over the last ten years or so!'

'Come with me!' I exclaimed.

I led Mrs Gray, with Alice and Jane in tow, to my three year old silver-coloured Rover. I sprang the central locking with the door key and opened the driver's door. 'This is the lever to operate the lights,' I said, turning the switch in a clockwise direction to illuminate the parking lot.

'Reverse gear is across and down.'

Mrs Gray stood transfixed, like a rabbit caught in the glare of a car's headlights.

'Here are the keys. Have a safe journey!'

As I placed the car keys in her hand, Mrs Gray seemed to come out of her trance.

'Are you sure you want to lend me your car?' she asked. 'How are you going to get home?'

'Don't worry about me!' I said. 'I have another vehicle.'

I watched Mrs Gray reverse out of the parking lot and proceed down the school drive. There was no crunching of gears and she disappeared smoothly out of the drive and onto the main road. I checked with Sid that everything was in order and then climbed into the twelve-seater minibus which the school had hired for transporting the chess players to the Tournament the following day. By now it was well past midnight and the main road to Boston was very quiet. After twenty minutes of driving the minibus as fast as I dared, I arrived outside my flat. Locking the van, I raced up the short flight of concrete steps and felt in my pockets for the apartment keys. My fingers grasped thin air; there were no objects in either pocket. It took a few seconds for the full implications of the situation to sink in, but then my heart sank. I remembered that my keys were in the glove compartment of my Rover. *What was to be done?* A further devastating fact came to light: I had no idea where Mrs Gray lived!

I vaguely remembered Jane saying that she lived down 'Cherry Walk', but where on earth was Cherry Walk?

Most people finding themselves locked out of their house in the early hours of the morning may have panicked, but my brother Gareth and I had constantly amused ourselves as teenage children by putting ourselves into imaginary dangerous or difficult situations and deciding how we would cope. Some of our solutions to tricky situations may have been a trifle bizarre but the whole exercise did develop a keen sense of inventive logic when coping with adversity! So I did not panic when finding myself locked out of my flat in the early hours of Saturday morning.

'*Let's keep calm!*' I told myself. '*I'll go through all the possible options and choose the best one*: *I could break into the flat by smashing one of the panes of glass in the door; I could ask the police if they could break into my flat; I could try to find Mrs Gray's house; I could sleep overnight in the minibus.*'

These thoughts came readily into my head and I swiftly decided that the easiest and least complicated option was to sleep in the minibus overnight and then to find Mrs Gray's house in the morning. I felt a lot more relaxed now that the immediate crisis was over and quickly returned to the minibus to try and grab a few hours' sleep.

There was plenty of room to stretch out my full six feet and the seats were reasonably comfortable, but it was a cold, cloudless

November evening and try as hard as I might I just could not fall asleep. Half an hour passed and I gave up. By now, I was getting exasperated with myself for being so careless. It was time for option two: I would drive to the local Police station and ask if they could break into my flat.

The officer on duty at 1.00 am in the morning was busy filling in forms. He paused, looking up to enquire how he could help. I explained my predicament and asked if anyone in the CID department would be able to break into the flat by using skeleton keys.

'What sort of lock are we talking about here?' asked the officer, 'Yale or Mortise?'

'Both,' I said hopefully.

'I'm afraid you've been watching too much television,' said the officer. 'We might be able to crack the odd Yale lock but not a Mortise lock. One of our officers could let you in by breaking a window,' he added helpfully.

I declined this invitation and thanking the officer walked wearily to the van. My spirits were beginning to reach a very low ebb. As I started the engine for the umpteenth time a startling new idea came into my head. I could drive back to Stickney and sleep at the school. I realised, by now, that I was not going to get many hours' rest but at least the school had a comfortable bed in the medical room and the heating would still be on. Moreover, I did have a key to the back door entrance of the school. This plan had the added advantage that I would be awoken early in the morning when Sid arrived to finish his cleaning operation. This would give me the necessary time to track down Mrs Gray's house in Boston. So, the die was cast. I rapidly drove back to Stickney, parked the minibus in the drive and entered the school by the back door.

Fortunately, the school had not yet fitted burglar alarms, so there was no risk of waking nearby residents who might suspect an intruder was trying to enter the school and ring the police. The medical room door was open and I crashed out fully clothed on the bed.

I was awoken in the early hours of the morning by the sound

of whistling. Sid had arrived and was sweeping the corridor that ran alongside the medical room. He was just reaching the final crescendo of 'Danny Boy' when I rather inconsiderately opened the door of the medical room.

Many months later when recounting the tale to my friends, I was willing to swear that Sid was so startled by my appearance that his feet left the floor by at least six inches. In fact, Sid admitted that at first he thought he was witnessing an appearance of the school ghost! Ever since one of the pupils had been killed by falling from the top flight of stairs, there were rumours of ghostly appearances in various parts of the school building.

I apologised profusely for startling Sid and briefly explained the reason for my overnight stay in the medical room. I asked Sid if he knew where Cherry Walk was and was greatly reassured when Sid was able to give its exact location in Boston. Not only did he know this vital piece of information but he also provided me with a phone directory which listed the Gray's residence as number forty-four. With soaring spirits I dashed off to the minibus, started the engine and headed for Cherry Walk.

On arrival outside number forty-four, my euphoric state began rapidly to evaporate. There was no sign of my silver Rover! Parked on the drive was a green Mini. This was mildly disconcerting as was the lack of any visible signs of the residents. I guessed they were having a lie-in. But desperation overcame my desire to leave them in peace and I rang the doorbell. An elderly lady with dishevelled hair opened the door slightly and asked me what I wanted. She was not rude, but neither was her tone overly friendly. I explained that I thought Mrs Gray lived here and that I urgently needed to get in contact with her as she had my apartment key. The lady had obviously just aroused from slumber and took several seconds to comprehend what I was saying. 'Oh, yes,' she said, 'she **used** to live here. We bought the property from her.'

My high spirits returned with the certain knowledge that this elderly lady would be able to direct me to my goal. Unbelievably, the lady did not have any contact address or telephone number for Mrs Gray. She showed me a pile of undelivered mail that she was waiting to hand over once she discovered where the Grays had moved to. In desperation, I implored her to delve into her memory to see if she could give me any clues as to where to start my search. After several minutes of thought, the woman remembered that their new bungalow was situated somewhere on the main road running through Frampton and she asked me if I found it would I be kind enough to deliver their mail? Once again apologising for waking her so early, I promised to deliver the post as soon as I located the Gray's house.

I knew that Frampton was a small village and that provided Mrs Gray had not parked my car in her garage, I should be able to spot it very easily. This proved to be the case and ten minutes after leaving Cherry Walk I was ringing the doorbell of Number 6, Main Road, Frampton. I breathed a sigh of relief as I recognised the lady who opened the door.

Without time for a full explanation of the night's adventure, I briefly stated that my apartment key was in the car's glove box and that I needed to get into my flat to collect the chess sets for the Junior County Chess Tournament before driving to Stickney to pick up the William Lovell entrants. I handed over her mail, declined the offer of a coffee, tempting though it was, grabbed my apartment key from my car, returned the car keys to Mrs Gray and within minutes was speeding on my way back to Boston in the minibus, waving farewell out of the driver's window as I sped off. My last recollection of the flying visit was a fleeting glance of a bewildered Mrs Gray slowly re-entering her front door.

Remarkably, I arrived at the William Lovell School five minutes earlier than the time I had scheduled to meet the six competing pupils. I was back on track, albeit harassed and tired.

The Tournament was to be held at Skegness, a seaside town about twenty miles from Stickney. By now, I knew the entire road network around Stickney and had no need to use the busy main roads. The Fens were drained by inter connecting dykes and drains and a series of minor roads ran alongside these drainage channels. They were mostly straight, but the surface was often very uneven due to subsidence, as it was difficult to build secure foundations on the soft soil reclaimed from the sea. I was in no rush and as I drove leisurely along I reminisced about the time the previous year when I was driving to Skegness and the garage had put out a police alert for the minibus I was driving!

The owners of the garage next to the school were two brothers, Ken and Graham. Both of them had joined the badminton club and had become close friends of mine. They were grateful for the business that I generated by hiring one of their minibuses for school badminton and chess matches. Their rates for hiring vehicles were very competitive and I was pleased that I could help them in this way. But the downside of the situation was that the brothers may have taken a slight advantage of the friendship to be less than efficient when it came to having the minibus ready and waiting! On several occasions I had to collect the minibus from a field half a mile away from the garage, fill it with diesel and check the oil and screen wash before I could set off. During one of the badminton club nights I raised this issue with Ken and was assured that the situation would improve.

The next Saturday following my informal complaint to Ken, the annual County Junior Chess Tournament was to take place and I had arrived at the school gates at eight fifty-five on a bitterly cold November day to see the minibus on the side of the road with the engine running. Hardly believing what I saw, I ushered the six pupils into the warm interior of the minibus and set off for Skegness. Little did I realise that the minibus in question was not the one intended for the school's trip to Skegness. Ken had hired out this particular vehicle for a trip to Manchester airport!

Having shown the customer how to operate the van, Ken had left the engine running and returned to his office with the client, to sort out the paperwork. Five minutes later, when he emerged from the office the minibus had disappeared into thin air! He shouted to Graham in the workshop and they exchanged a few choice words! Ken found it difficult to believe that Graham had no knowledge of what had happened to the minibus. After driving frantically down the main road for half a mile in both directions, they concluded that the minibus had been stolen and called the police.

I arrived at Skegness, blissfully unaware of all the panic going on at Stickney and it was only when I returned the minibus to the garage at six o'clock that the full picture became clear!

Coming back to the present, as I was driving back from the tournament, I was chatting to the pupils and was delighted to hear that one of them had won the Under Sixteen section and one was runner-up in the Under Fourteen section. I felt pleased that the day had been so rewarding for them. Competing against Grammar school pupils and defeating them at an intellectual game like chess did wonders for the confidence and esteem of my Secondary Modern pupils.

Chapter Thirteen: Contact!

Tempest's Garage didn't need the minibus returning until Monday morning, but if I waited until Monday to return it I would need transportation home after school finished at 3.45pm. In the circumstances, I decided that Sunday would be a much better day to complete the logistics of returning the van and ensuring I had a ride back to my flat. Furthermore, what better excuse for trying to see Jane again? I would ask Mrs Gray if she could drive my car to Stickney whilst I drove the minibus and then once the van had been left at the garage, I could give her a lift back to her house in Frampton. I felt certain I could persuade Jane to go with us.

After a light breakfast of cereals, toast and coffee, I prepared myself for the ride to Frampton. I didn't want to arrive too early because many people enjoy a lie-in on a Sunday morning, but I wanted to make sure that the whole operation could be completed in time for Sunday lunch. After a certain amount of deliberation, I decided that arriving at 10.30am would be the optimum time.

There was virtually no traffic on the road when I left my flat; the only cars I met were ones containing footballers heading for their Sunday morning fixtures. I soon reached Frampton. I rang the doorbell of No 6 with considerable anticipation and excitement! Possibly Jane would answer its summons! No such luck! Mrs Gray appeared in dressing gown and slippers and invited me in for a hot drink.

'By the way,' she said, 'my name is Angela. Would you like a tea or coffee?'

'Coffee, two sugars and milk,' I replied.

As I chewed on the chocolate biscuit and sipped the coffee, I was hoping that Jane might appear at any moment, but there was no sign of her.

I explained my transportation problem and Angela was only

too willing to be of assistance. After all, my generosity had solved her desperate plight at midnight on the Friday evening.

'I'll just throw on some clothes!' she said, 'and we'll be on our way.'

Trying to sound as casual as possible, I enquired, 'Is Jane around?' Angela smiled. She totally read the situation. 'She's still in bed, but I'll call her.'

'OK,' I said 'I'll wait outside.'

As she exited the bungalow, Jane headed straight for the passenger door of the minibus.

Despite driving at half my usual speed, the journey to Stickney seemed to pass incredibly quickly. I managed to ask Jane about the boy she was with at the dance. She informed me that he was her boyfriend but she wanted to ditch him.

'What do you mean, you **want** to ditch him? If you want to, why don't you?'

'Because it's complicated,' said Jane. 'If I ditch him, he won't accept it. He'll probably beat me up. You do know he's a boxer, don't you?'

I admitted that I had no idea. I sympathised with Jane's position and genuinely wanted to help her.

I blurted out: 'I'll help you deal with the boyfriend!'

Jane did not reply. When she next spoke, I was taken aback by what she had to say.

'You do realise that Mum fancies you and is waiting for you to ask her out. Why don't you go out with her?'

This possibility had never entered my head.

We duly arrived at Stickney and I parked the minibus on the garage forecourt as instructed by Ken and posted the keys through their office letterbox. The return journey was unremarkable. Angela talked about the cost of running her car and expressed doubts that she would have the money for the latest breakdown repairs. I politely agreed that the price of keeping vehicles on the road was becoming prohibitive. I offered to call in a favour from Ken and Graham and see if they could carry out the repairs on her car as cheaply as possible. Angela was very grateful. 'Would you do that for me? You have already done more than enough, but it would be fantastic if the bill wasn't too high.'

Jane remained silent throughout the journey. On arrival back at Frampton, Angela insisted that I must stay for lunch. I made a feeble attempt to decline the invitation on the grounds that I was a vegetarian and it would create too much trouble. But Angela would not be deterred by such a feeble excuse. 'I can easily rustle up a jacket potato and you can have the veg that I am cooking with the roast.'

I capitulated and was quite pleased that I would have more time to get to know Jane.

Angela busied herself in the kitchen, declining all offers of help with the preparation of the meal; Jane led me through to the living room where we settled ourselves on a comfortable, three-seater settee. I initiated the conversation by asking Jane about her father.

'Dad left home when I was six,' she said. 'He sends me birthday and Christmas cards with some money in them. Otherwise I have had no contact with him since he separated from mum. He is now remarried to Carol, our former next door neighbour from Cherry Walk.'

Another broken home, I thought. I had once carried out a 'straw poll' survey in the fifth year RE class and was amazed to discover that over 50% of the pupils were from single parent homes. Marriage definitely seemed to be on the wane or to put it more accurately, divorce was on the increase.

Jane seemed very philosophical about the home situation and at school had always appeared to be cheerful and full of the joys of living, so I guessed that the separation had not been too traumatic for her. *How wrong can you be!*

Jane had no brothers or sisters at the William Lovell and I had assumed she was an only child, so I was amazed to learn that she had three brothers, John and Jo who were twins and Steven. When I inquired why I had never met any of them, Jane told me that John and Jo were ten years older than her and both of them lived and worked in Lincoln. Steven was two years older than

Jane, but had been sent to a boarding school in Louth because Angela could not make him attend the local school. Just as I was absorbing all this fascinating family background, Angela shouted, from the kitchen, that the meal was ready and we adjourned to the dining room.

The meal was excellent and as a bachelor I was always very appreciative of having meals cooked for me. During the meal Angela asked me why I was a vegetarian. I had been asked this question many times in my life and I had a variety of answers depending on the reason behind the question. My intuition told me that Angela was not merely asking to make polite conversation but was genuinely interested in my reason. So I explained that I did not believe in killing living creatures and that I knew it was possible to live a very healthy lifestyle without eating meat, fish or poultry.

Once the meal was over and Angela had declined my offer of help with the dishes I thanked her and stated that I really must return to my flat to complete my marking and preparation for Monday's lessons.

Angela and Jane both stood on the front lawn to see me off and I hoped that it would not be too long before I would see Jane again.

Chapter Fourteen: The Strawberry Season

The lady members of the Badminton Club had decided to hold their fete in May when it was hoped the weather would be warm and sunny. Rather than book an expensive attraction they thought a junior, five-a-side football tournament would raise more money, as the mums and dads of the children would turn up to support their offspring and when not watching the football would spend money at the stalls. Flyers advertising the tournament had already been distributed to the local schools and football clubs and the response was tremendous. The school field was booked and many clubs agreed to run stalls selling cakes, hot dogs, chips and sausages, with others offering to run tombolas, lucky dips and competitions like skittles, welly throwing and pig pelting. I later discovered that this last named activity, 'pig pelting', had nothing whatsoever to do with pigs! It consisted of trying to roll a small ball through a hole in a wooden board situated about three metres away. It looked easy enough for anyone with good vision, a steady hand and good hand-to-eye co-ordination. But looks can be deceiving and the fact that the hole in the board was only marginally larger than the wooden ball, combined with the uneven surface of the school field, made the activity extremely difficult. It was a very popular local game as I was to discover once May arrived and the fete was held.

The women wisely agreed to let each club running a stall keep the profits they had raised. Each club paid a £5 site fee to put up their stall. Because of this, many clubs agreed to take part and it was anticipated that they would all bring many members and supporters. This proved to be the case and the ladies' conservative estimate of profit was well exceeded with over £1,000 being raised towards the new Village Hall.

A few years on, during the Summer Term, when school work became less intense, I felt that I needed some new involvement.

Almost on cue, a fifth year pupil called Tony Coupland provided a possible solution,

'Mr Shelby, have you ever thought of earning some extra money by selling strawberries?'

I was taken aback. 'No!' I admitted, 'It's not something that has sprung readily into my mind. Why do you ask?'

'Well,' said Tony slowly, 'My mother picks strawberries for a local farmer and I'm sure he would let you take some to sell. We could drive to one of the local towns and sell them door-to-door.'

I was thoroughly warming to the idea. I quizzed Tony about all aspects of the strawberry trade and was amazed to find how knowledgeable he was. I resolved to visit the farmer the coming weekend to see if a deal could be negotiated.

Maidman's farm was only five miles from the school and as I approached I could see the farmer disembarking from his tractor on the concrete area in front of the barn. I drove to the side of the tractor and alighted from my car. The farmer turned expectantly towards me and as he did so his face lit up with recognition. With a pleasant smile, he stretched out his hand, 'Paul Shelby, how are you?'

I had attended the same secondary school as John Maidman, but had not bumped into him since leaving! 'I'm very well, John,' I said. 'I guess Tony's mother told you that I would be coming.'

'She did!' replied John, 'and I wondered if it was the same Paul Shelby I was at school with.'

I had always got on well with John at school and we soon agreed a business deal on the strawberries. I could either pick my own and thereby buy them at a cheaper rate, or let John's workers pick them and pay a little more. John informed me that the strawberries were usually ready for picking by the third week in June and I promised to visit the farm again just before the harvest.

In the intervening weeks between my visit to the farm and the first selling trip, I meticulously planned every detail of the new business venture. I managed to borrow, from Ken's Garage, a medium sized trailer which could easily be towed by my Rover.

I selected four fifth year boys from the many pupils who had begged to become part of the selling team. Tony had been very useful here: he knew the pupils who would be capable of working long, hard hours and not get deterred by sales' refusals.

Tony suggested we would make a greater profit if we picked all our own strawberries and he assured me that all the chosen workers would be more than willing to assist in this task as they would earn more money this way. I readily agreed. By picking our own strawberries they would cost only eighteen pence per pound to purchase from farmer John and I was planning to charge at least fifty pence when we sold them to residents in Grimsby and Lincoln.

To make sure that the parents of the four pupils knew what was going on and approved of their sons carrying out this kind of work, I met with each of the families individually to explain the business venture and elicit their full approval. As most of them were struggling financially, the idea of their sons earning extra cash for the family was very well received. None of them voiced the slightest objection. As I intended to sell on both Saturday and Sunday, I told the parents that however tired their sons were from their weekend exertions, I would expect them to be at school on Monday morning. All the boys' parents agreed to comply with this condition.

The month of June provided hot, dry weather and on the third Saturday I met with my four co-workers at the school gates at 7.30am. We drove to the farm and were soon at work picking strawberries.

Many farmers who grew this crop placed straw between the rows of fruit. This had two advantages: firstly, it kept the berries from contacting the soil and thereby becoming muddy when it rained; secondly, it made it much easier and quicker for the pickers to kneel on the straw and pick the fruit. I was shown by Tony how to look under the dark green leaves in the centre of the plants for the ripest strawberries. My team of workers had soon amassed over two hundred punnets of delicious looking ripe fruit and I told them that they could now take a break whilst I loaded up the trailer.

Farmer John had his own pickers busily working in the field; their fruit was for other commercial buyers. When he noticed that I was ready to load the trailer, he strolled over to see how the operation was going.

'It looks like you could do with a few potato 'chitting' boxes to transport the berries in,' he suggested helpfully. 'You can fit exactly sixteen punnets in each box and that will prevent movement in the trailer. Help yourself to as many as you need, they're stacked over there in the barn.'

I gratefully accepted John's suggestion. The shed that John had indicated was full of potatoes, but in front of them was a large stack of empty chitting trays. I collected two of the wooden trays and carried them over to the strawberries. As I loaded the first box I realised that they would be ideal for transportation purposes. Not only did sixteen punnets fit exactly into the trays but the boxes were made of wood and very sturdy and stacked easily on top of each other. By the time I had filled the first two boxes and loaded them into the trailer, the four lads had finished their break and joined in with the work. The two hundred punnets were soon securely stowed in the trailer and we were ready to leave.

Just before we set off, I suddenly realised that we needed smaller boxes to carry the strawberries around in. The potato trays were ideal for transportation in the trailer, but they would be far too heavy and cumbersome for carrying door-to-door. I seemed to remember seeing some smaller boxes in the potato shed. Tony, always keen to be helpful, ran over to the barn and returned a few moments later with five small wooden boxes. He carefully placed these into the back of the trailer.

We pulled out of Maidman's farm just after 10.30am and headed towards the A16 and the town of Grimsby, sixty miles away. I had chosen this town for our first business venture because it was a fishing port with a lot of industries. I guessed that its distance from any agricultural area meant that the price of strawberries would be much higher than in the Fen area of Lincolnshire.

The four lads were highly excited and I had to raise my voice slightly to gain their attention. 'OK boys,' I said, 'now, listen carefully! Have any of you sold before?'

There was a deafening silence. 'Not a problem; it will be a doddle! Hard work but a doddle!... as long as you follow my instructions!

When we first arrive in Grimsby, we will check the price in the local shops and will undercut the lowest price on offer in any shop or supermarket. So you can be sure that our price will be very competitive! At every house where somebody answers the door, you clearly show them the box of strawberries and say, 'Would you like to buy any strawberries?' You then watch their reaction very carefully.

People will fall into three main categories: those who aren't in the least bit interested in buying strawberries; those who show some interest in buying and those who will definitely buy providing the price is right. Don't waste any time on those who aren't interested. Be polite and say, 'Thank you very much' and rapidly head for the next house. Those who want to buy will ask you the price and you tell them, making sure that you say that each punnet contains over a pound in weight.

The people who show some interest in purchasing a punnet are the ones that you spend the most time with. These are potential sales and it is your task to convert them into actual sales.'

From behind me somewhere, I recognised David's voice.

'How do we do that?' he asked.

'Easy!' I replied, 'You use your charm!'

The boys all broke into laughter.

'If we have to rely on David's charm, we won't sell any!' said Steven humorously, knowing full well that David positively oozed charm out of every pore of his body.

'Well, you can use a few extra facts to clinch the sale,' I added in a more serious tone.

'Tell them that they are freshly picked this morning and are cheaper than anywhere else in Grimsby. If that doesn't persuade them, nothing else will!' And remember first and foremost - at all times be polite, even if the customer is rude to you. They may not

buy any strawberries this week but if you make a good impression, they may buy some next week.

The small wooden boxes will hold six punnets. When you are down to your last punnet, return to the trailer and restock. Customers like a choice and seeing only one box may put them off.

If you have any problems at all I will be at hand to sort them out. Don't hesitate to fetch me! I don't think that there will be any issues but it is my job to sort them out if any arise. I want you all to feel assured and confident in what you are doing. Customers rapidly 'pick up' on the demeanour of the salesman. You need to be confident and positive at all times. If you've been turned down by twelve people in succession, you must approach the thirteenth house with the same enthusiasm and expectancy as you did the first house. Selling sorts out the men from the boys! Finally, each of you will have a 'float' and be responsible for looking after your own money. Any losses will be taken out of your wages at the end of the day! Once we've decided on the price, make sure that you work out how much change to give for the varying pound notes that you may receive.'

The four boys spent the next few minutes quizzing each other on the correct change to give for varying amounts of possible paper currency; whilst my thoughts centred on working out the best area of Grimsby in which to start selling. I had visited the town on a few occasions and remembered that near the fishing port itself were many terraced houses packed very closely together and with virtually no front garden. These houses would be quick and easy to call upon.

It took just under two hours to travel to Grimsby and by now the boys were raring to start selling, but first I needed to check the price in the market place and the local shops. I was delighted to discover that those shops selling strawberries were charging 75p for half pound punnets, and the strawberries on display were by no means fresh; some looking positively dull and drab. In the market, vendors were charging 50p for half pound punnets.

'OK,' I said, 'we'll pitch our price at 60p, and don't forget to tell them that ours are one pound punnets'.

I gave them one final piece of advice:

'Don't let the customers see you eating any strawberries, or they may think you are giving them short measure! If you want to eat any do so in the car but beware, I must warn you that if you eat too many you may get the 'runs' and that could prove very embarrassing!'

The boys loaded up their small wooden boxes and I wished I had thought of bringing some clean white cloths to put on the bottom of the boxes, just to add a professional touch, but despite this small omission the strawberries looked delicious and I expected they would have no difficulty in selling them. I sent two boys down each side of the street and told of them to visit two consecutive houses. In this way they would cover the entire street very quickly and there would be no overlapping. All I had to do at this stage was slowly drive the car and trailer along the street to keep pace with the sellers.

Tony was the first to sell five of his punnets and rapidly re-filled his box from the trailer and was on his way again. The other three boys soon followed suit and it looked as though the venture was going very smoothly. As far as I could ascertain about one in three houses was buying the fruit and for 'cold calling' this was a high rate of success. There was a lot of walking and carrying but I could see no way round this.

As they neared the end of the road, I decided to try my own hand at selling. After all I thought, it is no good telling the boys how to sell if you can't do the business yourself!

I loaded the remaining small wooden box and set off for the end of the street; by starting to sell here, I was certain that I would not encroach on any of my pupils' territories. I chose the opposite side to where Tony was working as it looked as if he would complete his allocated houses much quicker than the other three lads.

I achieved a sale at the first house I called on and was soon into my stride as a seller. At the second house, I encountered a middle-aged housewife with a very suspicious nature. She was clearly interested in purchasing some strawberries but needed that final convincing sales pitch. I told her that the strawberries were freshly picked this morning.

'How do I know that?' she asked in a challenging voice.

'Because I picked them!' I replied in a very confident tone of voice.

Ignoring my reassurance, she went on.

'How do I know that the strawberries underneath are as good as those on top?'

Not in the least perturbed by this challenge, I suggested that the woman should tip them out into a basin and check for herself. The woman clearly liked this idea and rapidly disappeared into her house, reappearing a few moments later with a medium sized white bowl.

I held out my tray containing the five punnets of strawberries and told her to choose whichever one she liked. She picked the one nearest to her and tipped the contents into her basin. I waited expectantly.

'OK,' she said, 'you're right! They are just as good underneath. I'll have two punnets!'

Not only did she purchase two punnets but she rang her neighbour's doorbell and when the occupant emerged, another middle-aged lady, she told her she should buy some strawberries. Two more punnets disappeared from my box.

When I returned to the car, the lads were all gathered around swapping tales of their successes and failures. Everyone was very elated as by and large their selling had gone very smoothly. Tony had sold nearly twice as many punnets as anyone else and it was obvious that he would prove an excellent salesman. Tom who was the most reserved of the four lads had only sold a dozen or so.

I told them about the incident with the housewife and the basin and explained to them that building good customer relations was as equally important as making sales.

'It may take longer to sell the strawberries today, but next Saturday it will be much easier as people will know who we are and trust us.'

As I drove the car towards the next street I reminded the boys that there would be no official break but they could rest whenever they wanted. All the lads had brought packed lunches, but Tony told me they would appreciate a stop at a fish and chip shop if we passed one which was open. Sure enough, at about 2.00pm we came across a small fish and chip shop on a side street. The lads rapidly alighted from the car and entered the shop. As Tony went past the trailer he grabbed a punnet of strawberries and immediately upon entering the shop started to bargain with the man behind the counter. 'How about a straight swap?' he suggested. 'One punnet of strawberries for a portion of fish and chips?'

I was amazed at Tony's bravado and even more surprised when the owner readily agreed to the barter! There was no doubting Tony's enormous business potential. I was delighted to have him as a worker.

The afternoon passed very quickly. There were no real problems, although I was accosted by two police officers patrolling by car. When they saw the trailer containing strawberries they pulled in behind where I was parked and leisurely strolled over to me.

'Let's see your licence!' said one of them.

'I don't need a licence,' I declared, looking them squarely in the eye.

'Oh, I see you've done your homework,' said the other officer.

They glanced into the half empty trailer and turned to walk back to their patrol car. Remembering Tony's business acumen in the chip shop, I shouted after them, 'Do you want to buy a punnet?'

The idea obviously interested them. They stopped in their tracks and turned, once more, to face me.

'How much?' they asked in unison.

'A special bargain price for officers of the law, sixty pence per pound!' I declared.

'That's a rip off!' said the taller of the two officers, 'We can buy them for fifty pence in the market!'

I always love this kind of repartee and knew almost as soon as it started that I would achieve a sale.

71

'Yes,' I said, 'but they're only half pound punnets; these are one pound punnets!'

'We have a real smart arse here!' said the smaller officer. 'Perhaps we should just confiscate his entire stock on the grounds they're contaminated!' After a little more banter the officers gave in and bought one punnet between them.

By five o'clock all the strawberries were sold and the lads were in high spirits as they sat in the car working out how many punnets they had each sold. I had brought along a small calculator to assist with this task, but all four boys preferred to do their own calculations. As I had already surmised, Tony had sold by far the most punnets: seventy-five in total. Next came David with forty-nine, then Steven with forty-two and finally Tom with twenty-six. I used the calculator to check that their totals were correct, one hundred and ninety-two. I had sold six. That made one hundred and ninety-eight and we had eaten two ourselves. Their totals were spot on!

Originally, I thought of paying each worker 12p for every punnet they sold but when I reflected on this, it seemed unfair that Tom who had worked just as hard as anyone else should earn only £3.12 whilst Tony would earn £9.00.

I decided to ask the four boys what they thought about the issue. They were unanimous: they should all be paid the same amount. I had expected Tony would dissent but he was very magnanimous and stated that it was a real team effort and that everyone should be equally rewarded.

I was keen to foster a spirit of loyalty amongst my workers. I performed a rapid mental calculation and decided that I could afford to pay each lad £10 for the day's work; this was to include the wages for picking.

The boys were staggered. Tom blurted out,

'Are you sure that you can afford to give us as much as this?'

'What about your petrol money?' added Steven.

'Don't worry!' I said. 'I've taken everything into account. By the way,' I added as an after-thought, 'I've decided to give Tony a £3.00 bonus for his outstanding selling!'

Everyone cheered!

The drive back to Boston went quickly and I dropped off each lad at his own house.

'See you tomorrow at the same time and make sure that you get a good night's sleep!'

After I had dropped off the last boy, I drove swiftly back to my flat in Boston to prepare for tomorrow's much more ambitious trip: to Maidenhead in Berkshire. The preparations did not take too long and I was soon enjoying a nice hot bath and a relaxing evening watching 'Match of the Day' on television.

Chapter Fifteen: We meet again!

The strawberry business venture went extremely smoothly; so much so that I introduced a Friday selling session, as well as the Saturday and Sunday ones. Friday was very hectic as the boys had to rush home after school, grab some tea, change and be ready for me to pick them up by 5.00pm. But there were no complaints from any of the lads or parents. Word of the operation had spread throughout the entire upper school and I was constantly being approached by pupils who wanted to join the successful business team. Some of the more enterprising ones, realising that the current team would probably not be available for work the following year as they would have full-time jobs, asked for their names to be put on the waiting list!

On Fridays we sold in Peterborough; Saturday remained Grimsby's trade and Sunday we travelled to Maidenhead. By now, the residents of Grimsby and Maidenhead knew when our team of sellers would be arriving and were often waiting at home for us. The customers were confident of the quality of the product and the word had spread that these strawberries were the cheapest you could buy.

One Wednesday evening I answered the phone and to my surprise I heard Jane's voice. Managing to get my voice under control, I said, 'Hello! How are you?'

'I'm fine,' she replied, and almost without pause went on to ask me about the strawberry business.

She had heard from one of her friends about the operation and wondered if she could join the team of sellers. My immediate reaction was to say 'yes', but another side of my brain was telling me to slow down and give the question some more thought. The car was already crowded with the four boys, their lunch bags and me. I doubted that we could squeeze in anyone else, even if they were as attractive as Jane.

Thinking quickly, I suggested a meeting to discuss the issue.

Jane had no problem with this and the following evening we agreed to meet at the Pincushion Public House at 8.00pm. I had deliberately chosen to meet at Jane's local pub, because this way I could talk in private. I intended to find out once and for all if Jane would go out with me and it would be easier to broach the subject if I was alone with Jane. I accepted that there might be a few regulars in the lounge, but from past experiences knew that most pubs were very quiet on week days and the drinkers that did call in often arrived after 9.00pm.

I liked to be punctual and exactly 8.00pm I pulled into the Pincushion's large car park. Judging by the lack of cars, I guessed there were very few people inside and this turned out to be the case: the lounge was deserted. The barman was busily placing clean, pint size glasses onto the shelf underneath the bar. He straightened up and with a cheerful smile said, 'What can I get you to drink, sir?'

Not wanting my judgement to be affected by alcohol, I ordered an orange juice with lemonade. No sooner had I placed the order, than the door opened and in walked Jane.

She looked every bit as attractive as I had remembered. She joined me at the bar and before I could ask what she would like to drink she looked me straight in the eye and stated:

'Mine's a double whiskey!'

I was taken aback! I had not seen her as someone who would enjoy the 'hard stuff'. But before I had a chance to order her drink, she added: 'Only joking! I'll have a coke.'

I knew that if I was going to get into a serious relationship with any lady she would have to possess a sense of humour. Jane fitted the bill perfectly! Could I persuade her to go out with me?

We sat in a corner of the lounge, furthest away from the counter, so that our voices could not be overheard; not that the barman seemed the least bit interested in our conversation as he continued to organise the glasses and optics.

I decided to deal with business first before raising the topic closer to my heart. I explained to Jane the logistical problem of taking on another seller at the moment. As with the drinks, she was quick off the mark.

'Well, there's only one answer: you'll have to sack one of them!'

Beginning to understand her sense of humour, I guessed she might not be too serious about this proposition. Sure enough, a second later she added:

'No, I understand; I'll have to wait until next year.'

To help overcome any sense of disappointment I pointed out that selling strawberries was highly dangerous work.

'How come?' she said.

'Well, only last Sunday we were down in Maidenhead selling in a street where all the houses had very large gardens, both to the front and rear; this meant a lot of walking. I was giving Tony a hand and we were working door-to-door. There seemed to be very few people home and when we came to the end of the avenue, we each still had four punnets left unsold. What made the situation worse was that the street was a dead-end and we were now facing a very long walk back to the car which was parked in an adjacent road.

Tony came up with what seemed like a brilliant idea: he suggested that we could cut through the back garden of one of the residences where the occupants were out and emerge close to where our car was parked. I agreed and we both chose a different empty residence to walk through. I walked past the house and headed down a small cobbled drive which led to the large back garden. At the entrance to the garden was a small latched gate. I opened this easily and moved ahead, little suspecting what awaited me around the corner. There fastened to a post by a long chain lay a large Dalmatian dog, fast asleep. In his slumber he seemed oblivious of my presence, so I decided to creep past as silently as possible. I had almost accomplished this manoeuvre, when in a blur of speed and light the Dalmatian, awoke, sat up and accelerated towards me. Before I could take any evasive action, it had bitten me on the buttocks and stood snarling and growling just a few feet away. Tony had heard all the commotion and was peering over the small privet hedge which marked the boundary of the two properties. When he realised what had happened he broke into in a fit of hysterics.

'It's all right for you,' I groaned. 'My backside is really painful!' This statement brought on a renewed fit of laughter. 'I just can't wait to tell the lads!' his words almost drowned out by his continued hearty chuckling. I finally edged my way past the dog without any further damage and Tony and I emerged from our respective gardens very near to where we had left the car and trailer.

Like Tony, Jane saw the funny side of the situation and burst into a fit of laughter. 'It's a good job the owners of the Dalmatian weren't in, or you could have been done for trespassing!' she managed to utter. 'I hope you had a tetanus injection,' she added as an after-thought. 'Some dogs can carry infections!'

'Actually, no I didn't,' I replied. 'I left it for a few days and it seemed to heal OK. Anyway, thanks for the sympathy!'

With this remark, Jane's features softened.

'It must have been pretty painful,' she said in a gentle tone of voice.

'It was! Sitting in the driver's seat was uncomfortable all the way back to Stickney and for several days afterwards!'

Hoping Jane was now in a more conducive mood, I said, 'Once the strawberry season is over in about four weeks or so, how about letting me take you shopping in Peterborough?'

Jane did not respond immediately and I expected she was going to refuse. I was therefore very surprised when she said: 'I've already told you, I'm supposed to be going out with Tony Pullis.'

I sensed a glimmer of hope. 'What do you mean by, *supposed* to be going out with Tony Pullis? Either you are going out with him, or you're not!'

'I **am** going out with him,' she said, 'but I don't want to.'

'Well, that's easy enough to solve!' I said. 'Ditch him!'

'Hmm,' replied Jane, 'as I told you, in the minibus, I wish it was as simple as that.'

'What's the complication?' I asked, getting more and more hopeful.

'First of all, he is living in our house as a tenant and would have to be evicted; secondly, he is an amateur boxer and would probably beat me up if I ditched him! He is a right psycho!'

I began to realise that a relationship with Jane would not be as straightforward as I had first imagined! I did not like the sound of this *psycho* boyfriend one little bit.

But, with Jane sitting in close proximity to me, all fears of Tony Pullis disappeared. 'You could move in with me,' I suggested. 'As a tenant of course!' I added when she looked a little shocked.

'I'm afraid I couldn't afford any rent out of my wages. I'm only on minimum pay,' she said. 'But it's a great idea, apart from the fact that Tony would come round to your place and beat you up as well as me!'

For the time being, I had to admit defeat. There seemed no immediate way round the problem of Tony Pullis. However, as Jane had not ruled out a shopping trip to Peterborough I was hopeful that at some time in the future I could win her over. For the present I decided not to push the issue. I had established contact and could always call her once the strawberry season was over.

I changed the topic of conversation to Jane's work and discovered that she was working at DCI (Dynamic Cassette International) a local firm that made parts for computers and typewriters. She was not particularly enjoying the work, but it did help with her living costs.

The next few hours passed all too quickly and before long the landlord's voice boomed out: 'Last orders please!' I offered to give Jane a lift home. At first she declined the invitation, on the grounds that she only lived just down the road but I insisted, saying that it was not a good idea for an attractive young woman to be walking home alone late at night.

'You know, you're very persuasive!' said Jane 'OK, I accept!'

The journey only took a few minutes and I was soon pulling up outside her house. As she climbed out of the car, she turned back to look at me and said:

'Of course, you could teach me to drive!'

Before I had time to think of a reply she had run down the short drive and disappeared into the porch. I drove off in a thoughtful but elated mood. I felt certain that eventually I would overcome the problem of Tony Pullis and offering her driving lessons would provide a legitimate short term solution to seeing her on a regular basis. Everything was beginning to fall into place.

Chapter Sixteen: Driving Lessons

As soon as the strawberry season was over, I contacted Jane and asked her if she had been serious about me teaching her to drive.

'Yes!' she answered very positively. 'Providing you teach me to drive like **you** drive and not the way the driving schools teach you to drive!'

'What exactly do you mean by this? Are you suggesting that I drive dangerously fast?' I responded.

'No, of course not, but you know what I mean; most of the driving instructors teach you to drive at a snail's pace, and wait forever at junctions before pulling out; whereas you look for gaps in the oncoming traffic and take advantage of them.'

'Very observant!' I commented. 'Yes, OK, I'll teach you to drive like I drive. Satisfied? We'll start your lessons immediately. We can practise on East Kirkby airfield.'

East Kirkby was a disused airfield from the Second World War and still had many of its original runways intact. A narrow public road ran through the old airfield connecting East Kirkby with Stickford. On either side of this minor road there were two runways. These were ideal for teaching the basic driving skill as there was no traffic to cope with whilst learning to handle the car.

Some parts of the airfield had been sold and acquired by developers as factory sites, but there was still enough untouched runway left for practising gear control, reversing, parking and emergency stopping. So the following Saturday, I put Jane through her paces on the tarmac where, not so long ago, the famous Lancaster bombers had set off for dangerous missions over Germany.

Jane proved a very capable pupil. She was enthusiastic and quick to learn the basic skills. I had her travelling up and down the runway, changing through the gears from first to fourth and back again. I taught her how to move slowly as in heavy traffic and started working on reversing in a straight line. I was very satisfied with her progress during the two hour lesson and felt sure that it would not take her long to pass her driving test.

I resolved to bring a few plastic cones next time so that she could practise reversing into small spaces. The school PE department had plenty of cones which they used to improve the boys' football skills by getting them to dribble around them keeping the ball under close control.

On our return to Frampton, Jane invited me in for a cup of tea. Before I accepted, I checked on the whereabouts of the 'boyfriend' and was relieved to hear that Tony Pullis was working on a building site and would not be back until 7.0pm. Reassured, I readily accepted the invitation and we watched 'Home and Away' together on the settee.

The following Saturday dawned bright and fair; a good omen I thought as I drove to Frampton to collect Jane for her second driving lesson.

I was at the wheel as we approached the runways at East Kirkby. I glanced into my rear view mirror and I saw a small white vehicle in the distance, approaching at great speed. I realised that the vehicle was travelling far too fast to negotiate the approaching bend. I sensed that a calamity was about to happen.

'Look behind you Jane!' I shouted. I had barely completed the sentence, when the white van flipped onto its roof and skipped along the road like the Barnes Wallis bouncing bombs. It shot past my car and with its final bounce cleared the dyke which was to the right of my car and came to rest, on its roof, in a field.

By now, I had brought the car to a stop in the middle of the narrow road and turned the engine off. We were both a little stunned by the spectacular crash. I was the first to speak. 'I think that we should drive to the nearest house and ask them to call an ambulance.'

Jane had quickly regained her composure. 'No!' she said 'We must jump the dyke and see what we can do.'

'Do you know any First Aid?' I retorted. 'I don't; so let's call the experts and let them handle it!'

But Jane was not to be deterred! 'No, we must see what we can do to help!' As she spoke these words, she was already opening the passenger door and moving towards the dyke. I felt pretty helpless but reluctantly followed her, jumping the deep, narrow, waterless dyke and safely landing on the other side.

It appeared that the driver had been thrown sideways by the impact. His head and shoulders were outside the driver's side window, but his lower torso and legs were still inside. His neck seemed to be supporting the weight of the car and he was as white as a ghost with no sound of any breathing. Jane knelt down next to his limp body and checked his pulse. 'There's no pulse and no sign of any breathing!' she exclaimed. Her voice was breaking as she spoke and tears were starting to well up in her eyes.

'Well I'm not surprised!' I said, 'I wouldn't expect anyone to survive such a spectacular crash. He must have been doing at least 80mph when he started to summersault through the air. Let's go and phone for an ambulance and call the police!'

That seemed to be the end of the matter; there was nothing more that could be done to help the young driver. The folly of youth, I thought, driving far too fast to negotiate the right angle bend!

I was heading back towards the dyke when I suddenly stopped in my tracks. Afterwards, I could not explain what came over me, but I had an overwhelming urge to return to the van with the dead man's body sticking out of the window. Jane had not yet moved and was still in a state of shock. She was simply staring at the lifeless body. I walked to the back of the small van and seized the bumper. With a stupendous effort, I lifted it a few feet into the air. As I did so, the young man sucked in a life-saving lungful of air. I nearly dropped the car back onto his neck and Jane jumped into the air. It was like seeing a ghost come to life!

'He's alive!' shouted Jane deliriously, stating the obvious!

'Go back to my car!' I said, with urgency in my voice, 'and see if you can find anything to put under the van, because I'm not sure how long I will be able to hold it up.'

Jane sprang into action. Within seconds, she was over the dyke and rummaging through the boot of the car for anything likely to act as a prop. Alas, there was absolutely nothing remotely useful for the purpose needed!

'OK,' I said, 'then come back here and give me a hand. Between us we might be able to hold the weight until another vehicle comes by.'

Fifteen long, arm-wrenching minutes passed before the sound of an approaching vehicle could be heard. 'Thank God for that!' I said. 'I don't think I could have lasted much longer.'

'Nor I!' said Jane. 'My arms feel as though they are being torn out of their sockets!'

The approaching car seemed to take an eternity to arrive, but eventually it drew to a stop behind my car and three strong looking youths alighted. They looked into the field to see what was going on.

'Get over here!' I shouted, 'There's a driver trapped under his car!'

With the extra strength of three fit young men, it proved a very easy task to gently lift the driver out of his car and lay him down some distance away, with his head supported by a leather coat which I had conveniently found in his passenger seat.

Although the man's breathing was now more regular, he had not regained consciousness. He urgently needed hospital care. Meanwhile, another car had arrived on the narrow road and its elderly occupants were rapidly dispatched to the nearby house to call for an ambulance and the police.

The four of us flipped the mini-van back onto its wheels and I noted that the vehicle which had so nearly taken the man's life was a small, white Ford Fiesta. Whilst we waited for the ambulance to arrive, Jane and I had to tell the enraptured audience exactly what had happened. By the time we had finished, we heard the wailing of an ambulance siren and a few minutes later saw the vehicle approaching from the direction of Boston.

The ambulance had a crew of two and they worked with extreme care and speed. Within no time, the young driver was lifted onto a stretcher, carried across the dyke and loaded into the back of the ambulance. The crew were full of praise for the assistance that Jane and I had rendered the youth, explaining that the weight of the car had been pressing on the driver's windpipe and that if it had not been lifted off him he would have been dead within minutes. I silently thanked God that Jane had insisted on going to the driver's aid immediately. Without her determination, the young man would have died a totally unnecessary and avoidable death from asphyxiation.

The ambulance was soon on its return journey to Boston with its siren wailing once again. Not long afterwards, a tow truck appeared on the scene and removed the wrecked car. Everyone slowly departed and Jane and I found ourselves alone again on the road.

'Do you still want to have your driving lesson?' I asked.

'Yes, I think so,' said Jane. 'It will help me take my mind off the crash.'

I set out the plastic cones which I had borrowed from the school and we were soon practising reversing and 'three-point' turns. We were totally engaged by these tasks and failed to notice the approach of a police car until it drew up and stopped nearby. I had just been demonstrating to Jane the importance of close control of gears, accelerator, steering wheel and handbrake when executing a three point turn. I looked up and saw the police car parked a few metres away. I said to Jane: 'Stay here and I'll go and have a word with him.'

As I approached, the policeman wound down his window and leaned out. 'Does the friend of yours in the car have a provisional driving licence?'

I was slightly taken aback by this question. I answered abruptly: 'No!'

'Then I will have to book her for having no licence!' replied the policeman.

'Not on private land, you won't!' I stated very confidently. 'Plus, you haven't seen her driving.'

I was not as confident about this second statement because I was not sure how long the policeman had been watching us, but threw it in for good measure.

The policeman sat in silence, looking intently at me. Intuitively,

I knew that the police car had arrived to check out the recent car crash and the officer I was talking to did not have the least interest in booking Jane for having no licence. I was beginning to warm to this officer's style of operation.

'I guess that you are looking for the crashed car?' I suggested.

'I could be,' replied the officer in a laconic tone. 'Do you know anything about it?'

I beckoned Jane to join me and the two of us gave the officer a graphic description of what had happened. The officer seemed visibly impressed. 'I'll have to do some checking,' he said, 'but I'm thinking of recommending you both for a commendation.'

Jane and I were totally taken by surprise at this suggestion, but nonetheless very pleased.

'We were only doing what anyone else would have done,' said Jane.

But to me, the whole incident was nothing short of miraculous.

The officer took our addresses and phone numbers before driving off towards Spilsby.

Jane and I stayed practising for a further thirty minutes before we abandoned the driving and headed home. We jointly decided that we would call at the Pilgrim Hospital on our way home to see how the young man was progressing.

Amazingly, in hospital, the young man had regained consciousness and although he was still rather concussed, the only injuries that he had sustained were minor lacerations to the neck which had been caused when the driver's window had smashed on impact. After undergoing a thorough examination, he was released from hospital the following day.

Three weeks later on 31st July 1992, Jane and I were invited to Boston Police Station to receive our commendations from the Chief Inspector. We were each presented with a framed copy of a Certificate of Appreciation from Lincolnshire Police Force and we both had our photograph taken with the Chief Inspector.

Chapter Seventeen: Getting to know Jane Gray

The regular Saturday driving lessons combined with the incident of saving the young man's life drew Jane and me closer. I decided to invite her for a second time to go on a shopping trip to Peterborough.

However, when I picked Jane up for her next driving lesson, she raised the topic herself. 'Paul, about that shopping trip you offered me to Peterborough?'

'Yes,' I said, 'What about it?'

'Is it still on?'

'Of course, when would you like to go?'

'Tomorrow?'

'Fine by me!' I replied, 'I've very little on at the moment as the badminton and football seasons have finished.'

So the following day we travelled to Peterborough. We left at 10.00am to allow plenty of time to have lunch and complete all our shopping.

It was during our lunch that I raised the question of Tony Pullis. I was very surprised to hear Jane's reply.

'As a matter of fact, he could be going to prison!' she stated without showing any emotion.

I was staggered.

'OK, give me the full story!'

Well, about two weeks ago, Tony had invited me to the boxing club to watch one of his fights against an opponent from Skegness. I'm not that keen on boxing, but rather than turn him down outright and suffer another beating I put him off and said 'maybe'. He didn't push matters any further, so we left it at that. I'm sure he assumed I was going to attend to support him. A few days later my best friend Alice invited me to a party on this same night and I agreed to go with her.

When the party day arrived, I left the house early so he couldn't track me down and told mum to tell him that I had gone out for the evening. Of course he was furious. By asking around his mates, he found out that it was Alice who had invited me out for the party night. He was livid with anger and threatened to kill me but rather selfishly I blamed it all onto Alice.

On the following Saturday, he saw Alice in the Market Place. She was in a phone booth ringing her boyfriend when Tony spotted her. In a fit of rage, he opened the door of the phone box, grabbed Alice's hair and put a knife to her throat, telling her that if she ever again stepped between him and his girlfriend he would slit her throat. Alice was terrified and as soon as he left she rang her father Claudio, and told him what had happened.

Claudio is Italian and not one to cross in this way. One dark night, his mates caught Tony Pullis in a back alley near the Market Place and gave him a thorough working over. Not only did he suffer the pain and indignity of this beating but Claudio also reported the incident to the police; hence the court appearance and possible jail sentence.'

I was astounded and remained silent for a while. 'Well,' I eventually said, 'I guess that could take care of him for some time. Now that he is out of the picture, do you want to come and rent a room in my flat?' Jane answered almost immediately, as though she had fully expected me to ask this question: 'You know that I would love to, but what would the Headmaster, of your school, think?'

I had never even considered this aspect of the situation; as far as I was concerned what I did in my own time, outside of school hours, was nothing whatsoever to do with the school or anyone else for that matter. I was about to give a flippant answer but almost at once realised that some of the school staff might strongly disapprove of me living with an ex-pupil, so I gave the matter a little more thought before I replied. 'There is nothing illegal about you renting a room in my flat. Yes, some members of staff may disapprove, but I can handle that. I've always had a reputation for being different from the norm and provided that we are not breaking the law in any way, I can put up with any criticism that I receive. After all, I know that several members of staff think that my strawberry business is highly unprofessional; I tell them that if teachers were better paid, I wouldn't need to involve myself in money-making activities!'

'Well, I have to admit,' said Jane, 'it would be very convenient. DCI are quite close to your flat and I would be able to bike there until I pass my car test. At the moment, Mum has to take me in the morning and bring me back at night, because it's too far for me to bike from Frampton.

'OK, fine by me!'

I couldn't believe how well events were working out. I sensed that this was to be a turning point in my life. However, little did I realise what was in store!

Chapter Eighteen: Driving Test

During the summer months my silver-coloured Rover died a slow death. As the exhaust valves began to stick it became increasingly difficult to start the car and until the engine became warm it would frequently backfire. One fine August day it refused to start at all! It had been a good servant to me and I was sorry to have to part with it especially as Jane was, by now, very accomplished at driving it.

I inquired from Ken the likely cost of buying a replacement engine and having it fitted, but ruled this out as Ken strongly advised against this action, pointing out that not only was the engine worn out but many of the other parts had similarly aged and could break down at any time involving a lot more expense. So I purchased a second hand Volkswagen Derby. Ken only wanted £500 for this ten year old car but assured me that it was very reliable. In fact he staked his reputation as a car dealer on the vehicle telling me that if I was not satisfied with it he would buy the car back from me in one year's time for exactly the same price as I had paid for it: £500! I could not refuse such a fantastic bargain!

Jane soon adapted to the new car and drove it even more skilfully than the Rover. She explained to me that reversing in the Rover had been difficult because the car had a bigger boot and it was therefore more difficult to judge how far the car was away from the kerb; but the Derby was much more compact and reversing was comparatively easy. She begged me to allow her to drive the Volkswagen on every possible occasion. Within three months, Jane had clocked up an impressive 5,000 miles experience and I felt she was ready to take her test. I was pretty confident that she would pass the test first time provided she remembered to obey the speed limits and followed the driving school's methodology rather than that adopted by those who had passed their test. For example, the driving school teachers insisted on the steering wheel being shuffled through the hands when executing tight turns rather than the 'crossing over' technique used by experienced drivers - including myself!

Three weeks into February, Jane took her car test. I drove her to the test centre where we sat in a small cabin waiting for her name to be announced over the tannoy system. There were several other teenagers in the room and all seemed very nervous.

'I hope I don't get Williamson,' said one candidate. 'He's a right pig; he never passes anyone the first time!'

A few minutes later Jane's name rang out over the tannoy and a military looking figure emerged from a small office at the back of the cabin.

'Jane Gray,' he said in an authoritative voice. 'Follow me!'

There were sympathetic murmurs from those still waiting for their tests and I guessed that Jane had been unlucky in being assigned the dreaded Williamson for her test!

I helped myself to a coffee from the machine in the room and sat down to wait for Jane's return. I knew that the test took about half an hour and with five minutes to go before she was due to return, I wandered outside. I hoped to work out if she had passed the test by the expression on her face as she re-entered the testing station. Jane returned on time but her expression gave nothing away. I waited for Williamson to leave the car and then rapidly jumped into the passenger seat.

'Well,' I asked, 'did you pass?'

'No!' said Jane in a dejected tone of voice. 'Failed on the three-point turn!'

'Never mind,' I said, 'there's always next time.'

Jane drove out of the centre and back towards her house. Before she had travelled more than a few hundred metres she stopped the car and asked me to take over driving. Thinking that she was too upset to continue driving, I sadly agreed to the request and wearily climbed out of the passenger seat to walk round to the driver's side of the car. Meanwhile Jane raced to the back of the car and then to the front ripping off the 'L' plates as she shot past me. I was bewildered.

'Got you!' she said. 'I passed!!'

'You wait!' I said. 'I'll get my own back later!' Then I added as an afterthought, 'Well done! Can you go out with me this evening to celebrate?'

That evening we drove out to a small country pub just north of Horncastle and drank a bottle of Pomagne between us. I had taught Jane how to play backgammon and she was more than a match for me! It was well past eleven o'clock before we left the pub to return to Boston.

In March Jane left DCI and applied for a job selling accident insurance for an American company, CICA (Combined Insurance Company of America). Jane had to attend a two week training course at York and pass an exam before being permitted to sell their products to clients. Along with several other trainees she found the training very intensive and had difficulty in remembering some of the presentation techniques. Her tutor Murray was very patient with his protégés and coaxed them through all their problems; only two of the original eighteen entrants failed to complete the course successfully. Her first manager in this new career was Allan Marshall, an ex-pupil from the William Lovell School, well known by me because we encountered each other once a month at County Chess matches.

Jane quickly gained success in her new selling role, some weeks earning vast sums of money, more money than I earned in a month! The downside of working for CICA was that there was no basic wage, everything was commission based. The highly successful weeks had to be balanced with the weeks when, try as hard as she might, Jane couldn't even give a policy away! The work also involved a lot of travelling with the unavoidable high cost of petrol. I quickly realised that to make a career as a sales person with this company one needed to be highly organised and disciplined, but Jane struggled in these departments! She went on extravagant spending sprees when the money was rolling in and kept no reserves for the lean times.

Chapter Nineteen: Revelations!

Jane had moved into my flat and was renting my spare room. Within a few weeks we had settled into a steady routine. One day I arrived home from school and made myself my customary cup of tea. I was always very thirsty by the time I had driven the eleven miles or so from the school, because there was no afternoon break and this meant teaching non-stop for over two hours without a drink.

Shortly after I finished browsing through the paper, Jane arrived home and I made her a cup of tea. We idly chatted about the main events at our different work places. Jane was far more interested in listening to my account than she was in telling me about her day.

'Mine has been a boring old day and I have only sold one policy!'

'At least you don't have any dreaded marking to do with *your job*!' I quipped. 'That's enough to depress anyone!'

Jane laughed.

'Talking of marking,' I said, 'I'm just going to nip out to the car to fetch a load in.'

As I lifted the boot to collect the year nine books for marking, out of the corner of my eye I saw a man approaching. I straightened up to see the unmistakable, squat, muscular figure of Tony Pullis standing a few metres away. Before I had a chance to say a word, Tony blurted out: 'I want to see Jane! Get her down to see me!'

I could see why Tony was doing very well as a boxer. He looked in fine shape and in different circumstances I would have been very nervous about the outcome of this encounter.

'You can only see her if she wants to see you,' I said in a confidently controlled voice.

'If you don't let me see her, me and the boys will come round and sort you out!' responded Tony in an aggressive manner.

'I don't think so,' I said. 'You will only come round if I invite you and I have no plans to invite you and your boys round here!'

Tony realised that his aggressive, demanding style was not working with me and abruptly changed tack.

'Look,' he said in a much more friendly tone of voice. 'I only want to explain to her that I didn't mean what I said to Alice in the phone booth.'

Jane must have heard our voices and when I looked across to the landing outside my apartment she was standing there silently. She was looking rather intently at Tony but made no move to descend the seven steps which would bring her on to the garage forecourt where Tony and I were standing. Looking up towards Jane, Tony pleaded with her to tell the police that he was a good-natured fellow who had no intention of harming anyone. Considering that Jane had been beaten up by Tony on several occasions, it was not likely she would agree to this. She didn't!

In desperation, Tony turned his attention back to me. 'Do you think that I will get sent down?' he asked in a voice that bore traces of anxiety in it.

'That will depend on whether the judge believes you or not,' I answered.

With this uncomfortable information ringing in his ears Tony slunk off.

Meanwhile, Jane and I were getting on extremely well. Jane joined the badminton club and we partnered each other in the mixed league. Initially we lost more games than we won as Jane was relatively inexperienced, but after a few matches we started to win most of our games and the other team members began to rely on us to turn in a winning performance. Badminton is a very social game and meeting many different players throughout the season helped Jane to gain confidence and self-esteem.

Two months later, Tony Pullis appeared at Lincoln Crown Court and was sentenced to eighteen months in prison for carrying an offensive weapon and threatening to kill. Obviously the judge had not believed his version of events!

The local Standard newspaper printed the main details of the case and Jane and I both read this. After reading the article Jane started to tell me about her early life.

It was from this conversation that I discovered some alarming, intimate details of Jane's past life. If the episode involving Tony Pullis had seemed dramatic, the revelations of childhood sexual abuse which I now heard were heart-rending and traumatic. Jane made me promise not to reveal any details of these terrible events that remained buried deep within her.

She was crying as she recounted what had happened and I was soon reduced to tears as well.

'What have I done to deserve all this?' she asked.

Through my own tears, I simply said, 'Nothing; you have done nothing wrong whatsoever.'

'So why have all these awful things happened to me?' questioned Jane.

I didn't answer Jane's question directly but instead asked her what had happened to those who had carried out these vile attacks on her innocence. I was shocked to learn that in all these instances nothing had been done to punish the offenders.

By this time Jane and I were so emotionally drained that we both settled for an early night. As I lay in bed trying to fall asleep, my restless mind kept returning to the revelations that I had just heard. How could Jane's bubbly, cheerful exterior hide such a tortured and troubled past? What a brilliant actress she would make! No one would ever guess that her lively, happy demeanour was hiding a soul full of torment and anguish. No wonder she became depressed from time to time! I decided that in the morning I must advise Jane to seek psychiatric help to overcome these terrible events, otherwise I was sure that they would fester in her subconscious and cause untold damage later on in her life.

The following morning both of us had a lie-in and when I finally surfaced from my troubled night's sleep and showered, I noted that Jane was still in her room. She emerged at midday looking as though her sleep had been as equally disturbed as mine. As we drank a cup of tea together in the front living room she apologised for burdening me with all her traumatic past.

'No problem!' I said. 'That's what friends are for. I feel I am now beginning to get to know the real Jane Gray, but I still find it hard to believe how you can appear to be so bubbly and cheerful with all these terrible memories in your mind. I didn't sleep very well last night because I kept thinking about what you said and one thing I feel very strongly about is the need for you to seek professional psychiatric help to overcome these traumatic events.'

Jane was non-committal. 'For the present, I don't want to re-live these experiences; I just want to forget all about them and get on with my life. As for how I seem to be so cheerful and happy that is just a front.'

'Well all I can say,' I said, 'is that you are in the wrong profession. You would make a superb actress and I'm sure that if you were on stage or in films you would have picked up several Oscars by now!'

Jane smiled and this is where we left the matter to rest.

Chapter Twenty: Holidays

Over the next few months I devoted a lot of time and energy into making Jane's new life as positive as possible. For her birthday I purchased £50 worth of shares in a company I had tracked for many years. It was one of those volatile companies whose share price fluctuated considerably throughout the year. It was currently at an all-time low but I was certain that it would soon be on the rise again and if Jane held on to the shares she would be able to sell them for a lot more than £50. To make the present more exciting, I hid the shares in my garage and then prepared a series of clues to lead Jane to their hiding place.

The idea of a treasure hunt to locate the hidden present proved to be a real winner. Jane revelled in the game! I had never seen her so animated before and I gained as much satisfaction from watching her excitedly work out the five hidden clues, as I did from winning some of my badminton matches! Once Jane had opened the envelope containing the shares, she immediately wanted me to tell her all about the stock market and what the shares were worth. I gave a brief account of how the system worked and showed her how to follow the company's fortunes in the Daily Mail. I also promised to advise her when to sell them, although I pointed out that once she had tracked the shares for a few months she would be quite capable of making her own decision about selling them.

I usually spent the summer holidays visiting either of my two sisters living in Canada; one was living in Toronto, Ontario, and the other one in Victoria, British Columbia. Both locations had their own attractions for me. Toronto was a much shorter flight and was reasonably close to the Niagara Falls and the Niagara Casino. The falls were spectacular and the Maid of the Mist boat ride alone made a visit to this area compulsory. I enjoyed the occasional gamble on the roulette wheel, the fruit machines and the card tables and for me the atmosphere in the Niagara Casino matched that of the finest casinos in Las Vegas. Victoria on the other hand was within driving distance of the Rockies, with some of the most awe inspiring scenery in the world. I believe that Lake Louise is the most beautiful place I have ever visited. Ken my Canadian nephew and I had once hired a canoe for two hours and paddled to the glacier which came down to the side of the lake. We alighted from the canoe and climbed a few metres of the slippery ice; it felt strange, almost eerie, to be standing on a cold, frozen surface when overhead there was a clear blue sky and the sun was scorching down.

This year, I planned to ask Jane if she would like to accompany me on my annual visit. I decided that Victoria would be the most enjoyable location for Jane. Delphine, who resided in Victoria, had no problem with me bringing an extra guest and said she looked forward to meeting Jane. Now all I had to do was to persuade Jane to accompany me.

Jane had never previously been abroad. She jumped at the chance to visit Canada although she told me she was a little nervous about meeting my sister. 'What if she doesn't like me?' she asked.

'Stop worrying!' I said. 'If the two of you don't hit it off, we can spend all of our holiday touring the Rockies.'

So with her mind at ease, the trip was planned for August.

The holiday was an amazing success! Delphine and her husband Stuart were excellent hosts, arranging several outings to local attractions. On one of these day trips Stuart hired a small motor boat and took us to Discovery Island. Here we saw bald eagles, sea otters and a secret garden containing cultivated fruit trees which had reverted to their wild state. Stuart informed us that the island had once been inhabited by a wealthy family who operated the lighthouse. They had lived in a luxury house, maintained a wonderful herb, vegetable and fruit garden and had imported everything else that they needed from the mainland. After the last member of their family died, fifty years ago, no-one had lived on the island. Their dwelling had fallen into disrepair and the lighthouse was no longer manned.

On the return trip from Discovery Island, Stuart told us that he would try to show us some killer whales. Jane and I were very apprehensive about the idea of getting close to killer whales in such a small boat but Stuart assured us that he was a local expert on these mammals and had regularly taken visitors close to these impressive pack hunters.

Stuart's technique for spotting the whales was simplicity itself: he used his binoculars to look for the large tourist boats which charged customers $50 dollars per head for watching the killer whales. Once he spotted one of these boats he gunned the engine, steering straight towards the sighting. He explained to us that the tourist boats used all kinds of expensive devices to locate the whales. He was simply taking advantage of their equipment and letting them do all the hard, monotonous work!

As we closed in on the tourist boat, Stuart slowed the engine right down and started to scan the immediate area with his glasses. 'Yes!' he said triumphantly, 'there is a pod of them over there!'

Jane and I turned our gaze in the direction Stuart was pointing and sure enough we could see seven gigantic whales speeding towards us through the water. As their bodies came out of the water, I could clearly understand why they were such fearsome killers; the speed and sheer size of them was enough to terrify anyone. Yet despite their frightening reputation I could not help reflecting on their graceful movements through the choppy waters. Stuart, in what seemed like total madness to Jane and I, now turned off the boat's engine explaining that the whales would not attack a motionless boat but had been known to overturn small boats that kept their engines running! We had to trust Stuart on this point as we had absolutely no knowledge of the habits or actions of killer whales!

The pod of whales came within six or seven metres of our boat but as Stuart had predicted they took no notice of the motionless object on the sea, passing by at remarkable speed for animals so large. Twenty metres or so past our boat they stopped and began to swim in large circles. Stuart became very animated. 'They must have spotted a shoal of fish!' he said excitedly. 'Watch carefully how they corral the fish before attacking!'

As we watched in fascination, the killer whales' circles became smaller and every few seconds one of the whales would break off the circling pack and dive into the centre of the swirling mass of fish to fill its gigantic mouth. It would then return to its place in the circle and a different whale would exploit the surrounded shoal. The feeding frenzy lasted no more than five or six minutes. Once finished, the whales continued on their course across the bay in a southerly direction. Jane and I were amazed how close Stuart had been able to take us to these terrifying predators, especially as the tourist boat had remained well over four hundred metres away and made no attempt to get closer. Stuart explained to us that getting close to the whales was all about anticipating the route the pod would take. Sometimes like today you came within a few metres and on another day you could miss them by the proverbial mile. Today he had been lucky and guessed correctly!

On the second week of our holiday I hired a car in Victoria and we took the car ferry to Vancouver. From there we headed for the Rockies.

We were soon in the Okanagan valley travelling along broad, well-surfaced roads, very different from driving on the busy English roads. We were surprised to find few cars on the road. We had no problem in stopping in the deep valleys, bordered by towering, granite mountains, to admire and photograph the magnificent scenery. We drove at a steady pace and around 4.00pm each day started looking for a motel for our overnight accommodation.

There were plenty of these with vacancy signs in their windows and Jane and I were spoilt for choice. When we spoke to the receptionist at our first selection we were overjoyed to discover that unlike in the UK, the price advertised was for the room regardless of how many visitors occupied it.

None of the motels provided breakfast but most had free coffee available at all times. I was amazed how cheap they were when compared to UK prices for similar accommodation, especially when you took into account their exotic locations. We took our breakfast and other meals at local restaurants although sometimes we would buy provisions at the local stores and make a picnic to enjoy at a rest area with breath-taking scenery as a backdrop.

Our outward journey took us through Penticton, Kelowna, Vernon and Revelstoke, with a slight detour to visit Lake Louise. Jane found this location as charming and beautiful as I had described it. Usually the mental picture one has formed from someone's description of a place bears no resemblance to the real thing but in this instance Jane assured me that her pre-conceived notion of what the lake would be like exactly matched the description I had given her!

As on my previous visit, we hired a canoe and leisurely paddled to the glacier. As we approached I could not help noticing how it had shrunk in size: the base no longer came down to the water's edge; it had retreated about fifty metres up the side of the mountain. It still looked spectacular with the sun glinting on the frozen, white surface, but there was little point in climbing out of the canoe as it would be far too dangerous to attempt to scale the steep, rugged side of the mountain. We satisfied ourselves with taking photographs of the area with all its beauty.

We made a leisurely return to Victoria by a slightly different route, stopping overnight at four different locations. They all had their own attractions but most enjoyable of all was the companionship between us.

Chapter Twenty-One: Gathering storm clouds

Jane stayed in my apartment for several years and our friendship became ever deeper. Jane became involved in the annual strawberry venture and proved to be a top saleswoman. Each year there were new faces in the sales team as very few of the previous year's team were available once they started full-time employment. Jane's CICA training gave her an added advantage when dealing with indecisive customers and she passed on many useful selling techniques to my young, schoolboy protégés.

To maximise the profit of the very short strawberry season, I included a visit to the seaside town of Skegness on a Wednesday evening. For this mid-week trip I didn't take any of the school pupils but worked alone with Jane. The caravan parks proved ideal selling venues as there was very little walking between the vans and the holiday makers were only too keen to buy the fresh fruit as a dessert for their fish and chip suppers. Selling 100 punnets of strawberries took no time at all and was extremely profitable. Many of the holiday makers asked me if I had any whipped cream for sale and Jane suggested we organise some small pots for our next visit.

Jane undertook the purchase of the whipped cream and very professionally visited all the local supermarkets to discover which one had the most competitive prices. She even managed to negotiate a discount on the fifty pots that she purchased. We jointly agreed to sell the cream only slightly above cost price as we were making such a good profit on the strawberries and it was important to dispose of all the stock of cream on the Wednesday evening.

The second visit to Skegness proved even more successful than the first one and within two hours of our arrival we had sold our entire stock of strawberries and cream and were on our way back to Boston. Jane was driving while I worked out the profit for our evening's activities. The June strawberry business venture provided me with enough cash to pay for both of us to travel abroad together.

Meanwhile, at Clacton-on-Sea in Essex, events were happening that were to have a momentous effect on Jane's life. Margaret her maternal grandmother was beginning to show early signs of dementia.

She lived in a large, four bed-roomed house with her friend Dolly who was almost totally blind. As Jane had spent many happy summer holidays staying with her grandma, she wanted me to meet her and so we arranged a mutually convenient Sunday to drive the one hundred and twenty-six miles to Clacton to visit the old lady.

I took an instant liking to Margaret. On her part Margaret quickly came to trust and confide in me. It was during one of our intimate conversations that I learned the details of Margaret's will. Jane was not present in the room when Margaret divulged this personal information and she made me promise not to tell any of the family.

On the journey home, Jane asked me what Margaret and I had been discussing. I gave a truthful synopsis of our conversation but omitted any reference to the will. I informed Jane that Margaret had told me she was losing interest in running the business units and was behind in collecting some of the rents.

Jane and I tried to visit Margaret every month or so and sadly noticed the deterioration in her physical and mental state. On two of our visits she told us that she had fallen down in the kitchen. When questioned about the falls she made light of them, chiding herself for being so clumsy in her old age. But Dolly gave a completely different version of events. She invited Jane and I round to her flat and once out of earshot of Margaret she informed us that Margaret's last fall had really worried her because Margaret had fallen down in the bathroom and could not get up again. Dolly had tried to assist her but Margaret was far too heavy for her to lift. Margaret had remained on the floor for some considerable time before Dolly could summon help from one of the business units. She felt that Margaret needed permanent home help.

Jane and I agreed with Dolly's assessment of the situation and informed Angela that immediate action was needed. After some discussions, the four Gray children decided that one member of the family should move to Clacton to live with Margaret and Dolly. The obvious choices were either Angela or Jane, as the remainder of the family were young men and it was felt that the two elderly ladies would not be comfortable with male relatives caring for them.

Jane was not keen to move away from Boston but volunteered to perform this duty if Angela was unwilling to do so. Fortunately Angela eventually agreed to take on the role of family carer and moved to Clacton.

Margaret was not without funds. At the back of her large house were six small business units and these brought in enough rent for her to live a comfortable life-style. She had not increased the rent for many years and the six properties were being rented out far too cheaply when compared to the rents for similar business units in this area of Clacton. Moreover, some of the businesses had fallen in arrears with their rent and Margaret had not bothered to pursue them. One successful lawnmower company owed over £3,000 in back rent and was making no effort to repay this.

On her arrival in Clacton, Angela soon became aware of the size of task she had undertaken. For the last six months Margaret had made no entries in her business ledger for income and expenses. Receipts and bills were thrown together haphazardly in a large file, along with letters from a legal firm Lowis & Co who were awaiting instructions on reclaiming back rent from two of the businesses.

Angela was already beginning to regret volunteering to take on the challenge from the business side of Margaret's life, let alone cope with the constant energy needed to look after two frail, elderly ladies. However she soon realised that there might be compensating factors for departing her quiet village life for that of a more hectic pace in Clacton-on-Sea. She was sitting on a gold mine!

Many years previously she remembered that council permission had been obtained for building houses where the business units now stood. With Margaret's increasing senility, she could possibly persuade her to shut down the business units and sell all the land for housing. *How much would that fetch in this day and age?* she pondered.

Whilst visiting the business units, one by one, her eye fell favourably upon the owner of a small company called: 'Town and Country Gates'. Over the next few weeks she made a point of visiting Sam's premises at least once a day. It was not difficult to find a suitable reason for these calls: she had little business knowledge and Sam seemed well informed of everything that went on in the units.

Sam and Angela soon became an item and before long had devised a plan to sell the entire area owned by Margaret to a local housing developer. Before this could happen, Angela had to persuade Margaret to agree to their plan.

John, Jo, Steven and Jane were receiving intermittent progress reports from Angela in Clacton but these briefings never contained any substantial information and no hint of Angela's real intentions. They were mostly stories of Margaret's declining mental health. On one occasion she had tried to pay the milkman with chocolate buttons. At other times she became very confused over peoples' names and identities and began to think that she was living in a hotel with Angela as a waitress.

Angela's children became increasingly concerned and asked me if I would consider taking Power of Attorney to run Margaret's business. They suggested that I should be paid for carrying out this work. I was flattered! I felt confident I could sort out any existing problems in Margaret's affairs fairly quickly and then run the business by making week-end visits to Clacton. I told the four children I felt honoured to be asked and would be willing to take on the task but would not accept any money for my work, requesting only petrol money for the weekly car trips.

Angela was informed of the decision by the children and agreed that this was a sound idea as all the family trusted me. However, she secretly planned to gain the Power of Attorney for herself. What better way of legally carrying out all her scheming plans? She rang me and offered to arrange for a solicitor from Margaret's lawyers to call at the house at a time and date suitable for me.

It was unfortunate that my appointment to arrange for Power of Attorney with Mr Lads, the Solicitor, occurred when Jane was out of the country on holiday in India.

The appointment could not have been more of a disaster! Many years later, when Jane and I discussed the chain of events which catapulted us to hell and back, we pinpointed this event as a pivotal one. On reflection I should have been more wary and suspicious of Angela's motives. She had agreed to the children's suggestion without even a single question being asked or a doubt being raised. It was too good to be true!

When I arrived at Margaret's house, Angela was sitting in the front room with Margaret. She told me that Mr Lads had rung to say that he was running slightly late but was on his way and would be with us in a few minutes. We were sipping from our bone china tea cups when Mr Lads walked in. To me he was the spitting image of the actor who played Bob Cratchet in a recent edition of "Christmas Carol" by Charles Dickens! He was of medium build, with curly brown hair and a boyish smile. He declined the offer of a cup of tea saying, 'Right, let's get down to business! Margaret, I understand that you want Angela, your daughter, to be given Power of Attorney to run your business. Is that right?'

I was dumfounded! I wanted to protest in the strongest possible way that this was not what the family had agreed to, but at this crucial moment in time words failed me. I left Clacton in a daze. I could not believe how easily I had been totally out-manoeuvred by Angela! Not for one moment had I realised how cunning and manipulative people can be when motivated by money and power!

On the Sunday, I left the UK and flew to Toronto to stay with Sylvia and her husband Ivan for my three week summer holiday. Although I always looked forward to these annual breaks away from the pressures of teaching, this year my mood was different as Jane was not with me. She had been invited to travel to Goa with Nicola her friend and chose to spend two weeks in India with her, rather than visit my relatives in Toronto, Canada. I suppose I should have realised that we were drifting apart and her commitment to me was fading, but all I could think about was the memory of the debacle in Clacton and this thought kept returning to haunt me.

I made a strenuous effort to relax. A visit to the Niagara Casino and an afternoon spent picking peaches and cherries on the way home, helped temporarily to divert the negative fears running through my head. Nonetheless my mind kept returning to Jane. How was she faring in Goa? Was she having a relationship with some handsome young Indian? What would she say about the Power of Attorney being in Angela's hands?

Sylvia and Ivan commented on the absence of Jane but I played down the importance of this, stating that she had been offered the unbelievable chance of a free holiday in India with Nicola and would have been insane to turn it down.

Jane and I returned from our respective holidays at about the same time. Although I was desperately looking forward to seeing Jane I was nonetheless feeling slightly apprehensive about how she would act towards me, particularly when she learned of the outcome of the meeting with Mr Lads.

My fears were justified. She was not at all pleased with the state of affairs in Clacton and blamed me for the impending disaster which she could already see in her mind's eye. When she lambasted me for my total lack of protest at Angela's duplicity, I could only meekly say that I felt powerless to intervene because I was not related to their family, but deep inside my heart, I knew that I had acted cowardly and felt ashamed that I had not mounted any challenge to her seizure of power.

The three Gray brothers soon learned of Angela's treachery and were as equally alarmed as Jane. Several times a day they were on their mobiles to Jane pressurising her to take some action against their mother to limit the damage she might cause with this newly appointed Power of Attorney. If I thought this situation was bad, far worse was to follow. Within a matter of weeks, Angela had sold the entire area of land which Margaret owned to a local builder whom Sam knew. Moreover, Angela had persuaded Margaret to change her will. She would inherit everything when her mother died.

I was not sure how Angela had engineered this last piece of manipulation, as Margaret was definitely not in a fit state of mind to make any rational decision about altering her will. I learned much later that Angela had continually worked on Margaret's vulnerable mind to suggest that it would be sensible to leave everything to her as she was now running the business and looking after her and Dolly full time. Mr Lads carried out the necessary legal paperwork to make the changes to Margaret's will. I seriously wondered how Angela had managed to convince Mr Lads that Margaret was in a fit state of mind to make such a vital decision. Had she offered to pay the legal costs in chocolate buttons??

Chapter Twenty-Two:
Margaret's Will & Jane's descent into Drugs!

After some serious reflection on the rapidly deteriorating situation in Clacton I decided I should tell Jane about the content of the original will. I started by explaining my promise to Margaret to keep the content of her will a secret.

'I now feel that I can no longer keep the promise I made to her,' I added. 'Angela's treachery forces me to break my oath so we can try and stop her in her tracks.'

Jane was somewhat taken aback by my revelation and was extremely curious to know the content of the original will.

'Margaret planned to leave half her estate to Angela and divide the other half four ways, with each of her grandchildren receiving a one quarter share. At a quick calculation, each of you would have received approximately £75,000 when she died.'

Jane was flabbergasted. She was silent for several seconds while she pondered this latest development in the Clacton saga. Finally she said, 'OK, what can we do to stop her keeping all of the money for herself?'

'We can speak to a lawyer and challenge the change in the will, arguing that Margaret was not in a fit state of mind to take such drastic action.'

Within a few days I had arranged to visit a local firm of Solicitors and speak to their legal expert on Wills and Testimonies. Mrs Nicholson seemed highly efficient and knowledgeable. She informed us that the content of a will could not be challenged until the person had died. However, in order to make a realistic challenge on the grounds of the benefactor being mentally unfit to make any change to the original will, evidence could be gathered and recorded.

So Jane and I described the rapid deterioration in Margaret's mental health that we had witnessed over the last six months and included in our analysis the latest, comical but heart-rending stories of her living in an imaginary hotel with Angela as a waitress, paying for goods with chocolate buttons and talking to George her deceased partner. Mrs Nicholson dutifully documented and dated these statements. 'I'll keep them on file until I hear from you,' she said in her brisk, business-like manner, 'and it would be very helpful if you could get her doctor to make some kind of mental assessment,' she added as an afterthought.

As the four Gray children contemplated the selfish, scheming actions of their mother, Jane's usually controlled demeanour began to crumble. There was no doubt in my mind that the deterioration in Jane's mental health was triggered by the situation in Clacton. When John, Jo and Steven learned that they had been cut out of the will they all turned on Jane and demanded she '*do something about it!*'

Jo threatened aggressive physical action against his mother. John and Steven remained calm on the outside but were inwardly seething at their mother's actions.

All three expected Jane to resolve the problems. Exactly how they thought this could be achieved was not clear; but sort it out she must!

The pressure started to have a dramatic effect on Jane. She could not provide the miracle solution they all craved and felt a desperate need to escape all the madness going on in her life. Crack cocaine seemed to provide the magical answer to all her problems. At first she only smoked a small amount of the drug. The adrenalin rush was phenomenal and all her worries and fears disappeared in the euphoric state of bliss brought on by inhaling the crack.

Over the next few weeks and months the addiction became stronger and she rapidly reached a stage where she could not function without her daily fix. I realised that something was seriously wrong with Jane as she was rapidly losing weight and her character was changing. As I discovered later, my guess that drug abuse was the real issue was correct. I confronted Jane with my suspicions, but Jane's addiction was now out of control. She was spending over £150 per day on coke which she washed up herself and smoked as crack. No way was she going to admit her problem. She intended to smoke herself into total oblivion until she died – she had lost the will to live!

As the addiction reached its peak Jane was incapable of carrying out a day's work and she stopped selling accident insurance policies for the CICA. With her income rapidly disappearing, other ways to fund her habit had to be found, so she resorted to stealing money from me. Whilst I was out teaching it was easy for her to steal my wallet and help herself to my money. Once that ran out, she used my credit card to take money out of my account as she knew the PIN number to my bank card. How did she know this? Well, I am a trusting person and remember Jane standing alongside me when I drew some money out of a cash machine in Greece, while we were on holiday there!

When I discovered my wallet was missing, I wrongly assumed that I must have left it at the William Lovell School or at the Badminton Club. It was not until I went on the Internet to check my accounts that I became seriously alarmed. There in black and white before my very eyes was proof that someone had stolen my wallet and was using my credit card fraudulently: withdrawals of £250 had been made on two consecutive days. There was only one suspect – Jane! She was the only person who could possibly know my PIN number.

I knew that Jane had a phenomenal memory for small details: she could recall the number plates of all the cars that I had owned since I had known her, including ones which had long since been crushed in the yards of scrap metal dealers! I surmised that Jane must have stored my PIN number in her memory and was now using it to devastating effect!

The bank was very understanding and co-operative. They put an immediate stop on the card and promised to refund the money into my account once they were satisfied the transactions had been carried out fraudulently. However, they were seriously concerned about the security aspect. They informed me that the chance of anyone randomly discovering the four digit PIN number was just over forty-three million to one! Therefore, the voice of the HSBC representative concluded, the person withdrawing the money must have been given the PIN number by you. The logic of the bank rep seemed flawless.

I knew that Jane could not have discovered my PIN number by trial and error. I therefore admitted to the rep that the culprit must have known the correct numbers, but suggested that at some point in the past Jane could have glanced over my shoulder and seen which numbers I had pressed. The bank official accepted my explanation and promised to order me a new Visa credit card and send out a declaration form about the fraudulent cash withdrawals.

After the incident of the stolen wallet I decided that I must confront Jane with my suspicions that she had perpetrated the crime. Therefore, on Friday evening after a strenuous week's teaching, I asked Jane to join me in the lounge. With a heavy heart I suggested that she had developed a serious drug problem and had stolen my wallet to help fund her addiction. Painstakingly I went through all the evidence that pointed to her as the thief. She remained silent throughout the allegations, then with her face contorted in rage said, 'Have you finished? Why would I steal from the one person who has done so much to help me? I'm not on drugs and I certainly didn't steal your wallet! You must be crazy to think that I would do such a thing!'

I was not convinced by Jane's denial. It did not ring true. I continued to push her to admit the truth.

'Look,' I said, 'I know you're on drugs. You're not eating properly, rapidly losing weight, not working and your character has changed dramatically - you are constantly restless and fly off the handle without any provocation whatsoever.'

In response Jane stood up, stamped out of the room shouting 'I don't have to listen to all this crap!' slamming the door as she headed for the stairway.

The replacement credit card arrived and I put it in the new black leather wallet which I had purchased to replace my battered and trusted one. For the first time I felt resentment against Jane for the loss of my hard-earned money, but more so for the loss of the four family photos which had been lovingly carried in my stolen wallet. These were irreplaceable.

I was finding the pressure of living with a drug addict in denial, very stressful. Trying to keep on top of the school marking and preparation was difficult enough with a tranquil home environment to work in, but performing these tasks against the background of Jane's deteriorating health and increasingly erratic, aggressive behaviour almost drove me to a nervous breakdown.

The second wallet theft was the final straw and through this incident I became aware of the depth of depravity to which Jane had sunk. Unbeknown to me, Jane had intercepted the early morning postal delivery and opened the letter from the bank which contained in it my new PIN number. All she had to do now to replenish her stock of drug money was to steal my new wallet and she didn't have to wait too long for an opportunity to accomplish this!

I was being much more security conscious about my money now, making sure that my wallet always went with me whenever I left the apartment. Whenever I was at home, I locked my wallet in a strong mahogany bureau in my bedroom. This precaution was very tedious, but my finances had taken a severe beating and I was fearful that the bank might not refund the stolen money. Moreover, I could not sustain further heavy losses without risking insolvency.

At this point in time, I was in the process of forming a non-profit making company to play the National Lottery as a syndicate. I had devised a set of rules and was working with Nigel, a friend from March, to design and print the membership cards.

Having arrived back from March at midnight, I was surprised to find Jane wide awake. She offered to make me a cup of tea and I gratefully accepted. I wearily collapsed into my comfy swivel chair and turned on the television to see what was on offer. As I half expected, there was nothing of interest. Whilst waiting for my piping hot cup of tea to cool, I decided to check on the Internet to see if I had any new Emails. My computer is situated in my bedroom and I soon logged on to my Yahoo site to discover that no one had contacted me.

On returning to the lounge, I drank my tea whilst skimming through the sports news in the Daily Mail. Over the last few months I very rarely had any conversations with Jane. She was either out, or she isolated herself from me in her room with the door firmly shut.

Before I retired for the night I looked around for my briefcase. It was nowhere to be seen. I vaguely remembered bringing it in from the car but was so exhausted I could not be sure of doing this. I asked Jane if she had seen it. She assured me that I was not carrying it when I walked into the flat: I must have left it at Nigel's house. *Damn and double damn!* I thought. *It is too late to ring Nigel now, I'll have to ring him first thing in the morning.* Then a brainwave struck me! My mobile phone was in the briefcase, so I would dial the number from my land line and listen for the ring tone. This way I would know if the case was in the flat; but when I rang the number there was not a sound to be heard; only a resounding silence.

At this point I gave up looking for the missing case and wearily crashed into bed. I soon lost consciousness and fell into a restless sleep, dreaming of Jane taking my second wallet and stealing even more of my money. I was addressing a bankruptcy hearing when I awoke. So vivid and realistic was the dream that I had a problem adjusting to the real world! When my mind became less clouded, I stumbled out of my room and headed to the kitchen to make a cup of coffee. I looked at my watch: 8.00am. Not feeling in the least bit refreshed by the night's broken sleep, but determined to track down my missing briefcase, I made my way towards the phone in the front room.

As I walked across the landing I was surprised to hear the front door open and see Jane walking up the short flight of steps towards me.

'Where have you been at this early hour of the morning?' I asked.

'Out and about!' she answered in a more friendly voice than I was used to of late.

I rang Nigel, my voice filled with hope as I inquired about my missing brief case.

Nigel was adamant. 'You took it with you when you left.'

I was filled with despair. I carried my mug of coffee into the bedroom and logged onto the net. Filled with apprehension I entered my HSBC bank account - another £250 had been siphoned out! In an instant, I knew where Jane had been in the early hours of the morning: using my new credit card to buy drugs. That also meant she had my wallet and my mobile phone. Would I ever see them again, I pondered? Probably not! Was it worth confronting her about the missing briefcase? No! I decided, it was not worth the mental stress. Jane was beyond all hope. She would die a drug addict unless I could get her to admit that she needed help. I had one last card to play.

Jane was losing weight at an alarming rate. The beautiful attractive female was rapidly becoming a bag of skin and bones. She was not eating any solid food and her face had a sunken withdrawn look about it. Her physique now resembled that of a starving African child. She weighed less than six stone and the bones were sticking out of her legs and arms. I decided that I might force a truthful admission about the drug addiction from her if I had evidence from her doctor.

She had visited her surgery recently so I asked if she would give me permission to speak to her doctor about her condition. Surprisingly, Jane agreed to sign a letter giving me permission to speak to her GP.

The visit to the local surgery confirmed my worst fears. Although Jane had denied taking any drugs, the doctor was one hundred percent certain that she was hooked on heroin or cocaine. He had seen far too many cases of serious addiction not to recognise the symptoms. He told me that her condition was serious and that without treatment she would probably live only another six weeks or so.

The doctor's verdict came as no surprise to me, but the confirmation of my own suspicion was like a bolt through my heart: Jane was determined to kill herself and there was nothing that I could do about the situation while she remained in denial.

On the half mile drive back from the surgery to my flat I nearly crashed headlong into the car in front of me which had stopped at the traffic lights. I screeched to a halt only a few centimetres from the driver's back bumper. The shock of the near miss brought me back to my senses and I tried to pull myself together, but my whole world was falling apart. Did I really want to go on living when Jane was dead? Nothing seemed to matter anymore.

Jane listened dispassionately to my analysis of the doctor's verdict and reiterated her former position: 'I am not on any drugs and I don't need you interfering in my life!'

I had already considered my options if she continued to deny there was any problem. I was in tears as I pronounced my decision. 'Then you must leave my apartment, as I am not prepared to watch you die.'

Jane was stunned. 'So you are throwing me out onto the street?'

'Yes,' I said, with tears streaming down my face. 'You have left me with no alternative.'

Within the hour, Jane had packed her meagre belongings into her black, Ford Mondeo and was heading south to Cornwall.

Chapter Twenty-Three: Arrest!

I tried to put all thoughts of Jane out of my mind but found it impossible to do this. Every day I expected a phone call from some unknown person informing me that Jane had died from a drug overdose.

Three days after she left I was surprised to receive a post card from Falmouth on which Jane had scribbled the address where she was staying. At least she was making an effort to keep in contact I thought. For a full minute my gloom and despair was lifted. *Perhaps she had run out of money and stopped taking drugs? Or possibly she had been unable to find a drug dealer in Cornwall?* This fleeting joy soon evaporated when I reminded myself of the reality of the situation. Jane was a drug addict in complete denial. She would obtain money by any means possible. If she had been able to steal money from me and I was aware of her addiction, how much easier would it be in Falmouth where no one knew of her problem?

Although I now believed that nothing I could do or say would affect the course of events, I nevertheless determined to make one last effort to influence Jane and steer her back to sanity. I wrote a letter:

Dear Jane,
What has happened to the real Jane?
Can you remember when, at sixteen years of age, we visited the Little Chef at Sutterton? After we had eaten our meal the bill arrived and I noticed that the waitress had forgotten to charge us for our Maple Syrup pancakes. I was not going to say anything about this, just pay the amount on the bill, but you were adamant that we must tell the waitress of her error. You even refused to leave the restaurant until I paid the money owing. You were so honest, much more honest than I was!

*Where has that honest Jane disappeared to? I don't believe the person living in your body now is the real Jane. The real **you** has been forced into hiding, because the drugs have taken over your mind and body. There is still time to change if you are honest with yourself and admit that you have a serious problem and need professional help. If you fail to do this you will be dead within a matter of weeks.*

Please, please, please ring me and admit your drug problem. I will sort out the professional help that you need.

Love, Paul

Three long weeks passed with no news from Cornwall. I began to fear the worst. On the Monday evening of the fourth week at 5.00pm, I received a phone call from Falmouth Police Station. The officer on the line informed me that Jane had been arrested for fraud and was currently being held in the cells at the station. She had shown the arresting officer my letter and asked him to contact me and inform me of what had happened.

Apparently, she had stolen a cheque book from a furniture company in the town and cashed a cheque for £800 at a local finance bureau. As soon as the cheque was presented to the owner's bank the fraudulent transaction was exposed and three, hefty Police Officers were despatched to Jane's Falmouth address. When arrested, Jane finally admitted that she had a serious drug problem.

The officer speaking to me seemed intent on finding an acceptable solution to the issue without having to resort to a prosecution in court. He informed me that although Jane had been charged with the theft of the cheque book and fraudulently using it to obtain money, the owner of the furniture store would not prosecute if the £800 was immediately repaid. Jane would be held overnight in the cells but could be released the following day if I could find a residential drug rehabilitation clinic to which she could be transferred.

At last there was a glimmer of light and hope! However, I needed to act swiftly to capitalise on this slight chance of salvation!

I thanked the Police Officer for his tolerance and understanding, promising to ring back once I had sorted something out.

For months I had been in a hopeless position where I could only watch Jane slowly and painfully try to kill herself with drugs. The frustration and sorrow had been unbearable. I had only survived by forcing Jane to leave my company. I did not want to witness her final painful and sordid end.

Now, at last, I could do something practical to try and save her. With a tremendous release of energy after months of helpless inactivity, I rushed to turn on my computer to search for residential drug clinics in the UK. I only managed to find one, situated in a village in Kent with a strange sounding name – Godden Green; I printed off their home page with the contact details and rushed to my land line to ring them.

The receptionist who answered had a friendly, welcoming voice and assured me that they currently had a few places open and would be able to help Jane, but their weekly fee was a staggering £3,000.

I spent the next hour ringing the NHS direct line to see what free help was available. I was disappointed to discover that they had very few residential clinics and the waiting time for admission was at least six months; even a psychiatric consultation would take several weeks to arrange as all appointments were made through the local doctor and resources were stretched to breaking point. So much for the government's promises to reform the NHS and speed up treatments, I thought!

There was only one sensible, realistic course of action: I would have to convince her mother to pay £3,000 for Jane to be admitted to the Godden Green Clinic. Having recently sold Margaret's estate for just under one million pounds, would she seriously miss a few thousand pounds?

When I briefly told Angela of Jane's plight at Falmouth Police station and her recent descent into drug addiction, she was stunned into silence. How could all this happen to her daughter without her knowing anything about it? Why had she not been warned earlier that Jane had a serious drug problem?

I pushed on relentlessly. 'There is not enough time now for me to explain everything that has happened over the last six months but I promise once we have sorted out somewhere for Jane to be treated, I will travel down to Clacton and tell you all the details.'

This statement seemed to satisfy Angela and she listened to my summary of what immediate help I needed to start Jane's recovery.

'I need a cheque for £800 to repay the money she fraudulently obtained from the financial bureau and I need a commitment of £3,000 to pay for the treatment at Godden Green Clinic.'

Considering the large amount of money I was requesting, Angela was surprisingly co-operative.

'OK,' she said, 'I'll put a cheque in the post tomorrow morning for the £800 and have the rest of the money made available when you need it.'

I gave an inward sigh of relief: so far so good! I had deliberately omitted to mention that the treatment at the clinic would cost £3,000 per week, not £3,000 for the complete programme!

At 7.00pm I rang Falmouth Police station and informed them of the arrangements I had managed to organise.

'Lucky young lady!' commented the officer on the line. 'She must have some very good friends! I wish every addict had her help and support!'

Then he added. 'She will be held here overnight and transferred to the drug clinic tomorrow morning once all the paperwork has been completed.'

For the first time in many months, I slept soundly that night and my dreams were pleasant ones!

Chapter Twenty-Four: Godden Green

On the second week of Jane's stay in Godden Green, I received a phone call from her. She sounded nervous and hesitant, as though she was not sure of what kind of reception she would get from me. Her character had changed; there was no longer the confident, aggressive tone which was prevalent during her drug addiction. Her voice was soft and gentle with a slight stammer as though she was feeling her way with a complete stranger. My heart went out to her.

'It's great to hear from you!'

'Next weekend there is a meeting for friends and family of the residents,' she said. 'Would you like to visit and attend?' She spoke with hesitancy and uncertainty, as though she expected me to decline this offer.

'I would be delighted to travel down to see you and attend a counselling session. I wouldn't miss it for the world!'

'I know how busy you are. I thought you might have something else on?' said Jane, as if explaining her earlier doubts.

'If I had, I would cancel it!'

My spirits were at an all time high. I had descended into hell and on the sixth month had risen from the dead! This was the second miracle that I had been privileged to witness: firstly, the saving of a man's life after a spectacular car crash and secondly, helping to save Jane's life when all seemed doomed to failure! How could I ever have doubted the power of God to bring salvation in the most desperate of situations? In silent prayer, I vowed that I would recount this amazing, true story to give hope to all families facing for the first time the reality that their son or daughter had become a drug addict.

The week passed extremely slowly. Time stood still and it seemed to me as though Sunday would never arrive, but at last I was driving south on the M11 towards the Dartford tunnel and my long awaited meeting with Jane.

The clinic was hard to find as it was situated at the end of a long, narrow lane flanked on either side by expensive looking houses. The surface of the lane had no tarmac and was covered in deep ruts filled with water. I remembered Jane telling me that the turn for the clinic was directly opposite a pub, but she had failed to mention that it was accessed by a farm track, covered in gravel!

I had found the pub easily enough but as I crawled along the dirt track I was beginning to wonder if there was another possible location for the clinic further along the village road? But as I rounded yet another bend in the track, I could see the grounds of the clinic stretching out in front of me. It was a very impressive sight! The driveway must have been over one hundred metres long and the neatly manicured lawns and ornate gardens gave me the impression of entering the residence of a wealthy aristocratic family. The clinic itself was housed in a magnificent ancient mansion. I found a parking spot around the side of the building, in what looked like an old courtyard, where, in times gone by, the owners probably stabled their horses.

As I walked back to the main entrance, Jane emerged from the front door. She had been watching for my arrival from the sitting room situated on the first floor. We embraced and hugged each other. It was a very emotional moment for both of us and tears welled up in my eyes. I knew that there was still a long way to go before I could be certain that Jane had finally kicked the drug addiction but there was no doubting the genuine change in her character: she had returned to the honest, vulnerable Jane of former years.

I found the meeting fascinating! The spacious room was packed with over thirty people from all walks of life. Those receiving treatment spoke first about their hopes and fears and then the friends and family were invited to contribute to the session.

All the residents were being treated for many kinds of addictions. They included addiction to food, alcohol, drugs and cosmetic surgery. I was amazed to discover that the resident suffering from dysmorphobia, the scientific name for an addiction to cosmetic surgery, was a male! It made sense to me that women might resort to surgery to maintain their youthful appearance or enhance their breasts, but I found it difficult to picture men with these same desires!

Liz, the counsellor conducting the session, asked the patients to raise their hands if this was their first time in a treatment centre. Of all those present, only Jane raised her hand. All had relapsed at least once! This did not augur well for the future I thought. But despite this evidence of the difficulties and pitfalls which lay ahead, I was not in the least bit pessimistic about Jane's ability to kick the drug habit forever. In my opinion, her addiction to crack cocaine was triggered by the actions of her mother in Clacton, but the real deep-rooted cause was her sexual abuse as a child. I was certain that once this was treated and her self-esteem was restored she would have no desire to return to the crazy world of the crack addict!

As the friends and relatives took their turn to speak, their stories all had a familiar recurring theme and contained numerous examples of lies, deception, theft, change of character, isolation and aggression. I could relate to all of their experiences and particularly empathised with their sadness and helplessness at being unable to influence the dramatic decline in the physical and mental state of their loved ones. When asked by Liz to express their hopes and fears for the future, they all feared another relapse. Their hopes centred on a final, lasting cure. I was the last one to speak. I stated that I had no fears that Jane would relapse, but hoped she would finally find the inner happiness that so far had been absent from her life.

The meeting ended and Jane took me upstairs to show me her room and introduce me to some of the residents she had befriended. These included Rose, a kleptomaniac, and Dave the guy who suffered from dysmorphobia. I enjoyed my conversation with these two people. My knowledge of addiction was expanding.

The afternoon passed all too quickly and as darkness descended I knew I must soon leave the clinic to start the long drive back to Boston. Jane came out to the court yard to see me off and we fondly embraced for a second time. But before I climbed into the driver's seat of my car for the return journey, Jane made me promise that I would visit her again next week-end. I happily agreed!

On the way home, I reflected on the day's events. Jane had certainly changed. She was no longer arrogant and sure of herself. It was as though she had reverted to childhood and was having to learn how to manage her life all over again. It reminded me of the time her brother Steven had been released from prison after serving an eighteen month sentence for theft. I had allowed Steven to stay at my flat for three months, sharing a room with his sister, until the local council Housing Department could find him a place of his own.

Steven found it extremely difficult to adjust to the freedom of life after having been institutionalised for so long. He would seek Jane's approval on everything, even the most trivial of matters.

'Is my hair OK?'

'Is this shirt all right?'

'Should I go out in these jeans?'

I found Steven's constant need for approval rather irritating, but Jane remained very patient and understanding with her brother and continued to give him reassurances whenever he needed them.

It was now my turn to show patience and understanding with Jane. It was not that she needed reassurances about her physical appearance or what clothes to wear, but she did need lots of support in the recovery programmes that she was undertaking.

She told me that when she first arrived at the clinic she was put on massive doses of prescribed drugs to wean her off the crack cocaine. She spent most of the first three days asleep in her room and when she did try to attend evening meetings she invariably fell asleep on her chair during them!

She confided in me she was very worried that the crack cocaine may have affected her speech and her memory. She was finding it difficult to remember much about the last six months of her life and would suddenly forget what she was talking about in the middle of a sentence. Liz had told her that this was a common symptom in the early stages of recovery from drug addiction, but Jane was worried that because of the excessive amounts of crack she had smoked she might suffer permanent impairment of these faculties. I impressed on her the need to stay positive and be patient with herself. 'After all,' I said, 'everyone will still love you, even if you are a stammering amnesiac!'

Jane punched me on the arm, but she couldn't stop herself laughing at my quick turn of wit!

Jane remained at Godden Green for four weeks and I visited her every weekend. I was pleased to learn that Liz was addressing the issues of childhood sexual abuse. Angela had been invited down for a consultation with Liz and Jane to discuss how the abuse had happened. Even Jane's father Michael, who had left the marital home when his daughter was only six years old, attended a counselling session to offer support to Jane.

Jane told me that the sessions with her mother and father were extremely harrowing. Since leaving Angela, her father had remarried and the only contact he had with his former family was to post Christmas and birthday cards to his children. Jane had not seen him since she was six years old and he in turn was totally unaware of the tragic happenings in her life. Liz's revelations reduced him to tears. He promised that henceforth he would ring Jane once a week on a Sunday and offer whatever support he could.

However, Angela seemed unmoved. Like Michael, her ex-husband, she had been unaware of the sexual abuse going on in her house. She never expressed any sorrow or remorse that Jane had undergone such dreadful suffering. She seemed driven by the desire to clear herself. She repeatedly told Liz that she must have been out working when the sexual abuse took place. Therefore, no way could she be held responsible for any of it. The fact that she had left a vulnerable young girl at home totally unsupervised, apart from her twin brothers who were only a little older than she was, never struck Angela as unwise. She was in complete denial of any responsibility for the sexual abuse which had gone on under her very nose.

Chapter Twenty-Five: - Recovery

Jane did not want to return to Cornwall once her treatment at Godden Green was finished, so she asked me if I would help persuade her mother to buy a cottage in Clacton where she could live. The amount of Capital Gains Tax and Inheritance Tax owing to the Inland Revenue from the sale of Margaret's estate had not been finalised and Angela's accountant suggested that whilst waiting for this figure to be agreed upon, it would be prudent to invest some of the money in property.

Therefore, Angela readily agreed to our suggestion. Pickle Cottage, a detached, three bed-roomed cottage near the centre of the town, was purchased. The asking price of £130,000 seemed very reasonable for a property which had recently been renovated and modernised.

Jane's treatment at Godden Green lasted just over four weeks. When she was ready to leave the clinic, everything fell neatly into place. Jane moved out of Godden Green and into her own home in Branston Road, Clacton-on-Sea. Because she was in recent recovery and slightly nervous of living on her own, she invited Dave the fellow patient suffering from dysmorphobia to rent a room from her in the house. Dave accepted her invitation and the two of them supported each other in their recovery from addiction.

During her time at Godden Green, Jane had become good friends with her counsellor, Liz Ellis. They remained in contact when Jane left the clinic and Liz became the rock to which Jane could anchor herself during the turbulent times of the first few months of recovery.

Liz had recommended that Jane should join a local AA or NA group and work through the Twelve Steps. I also remained very supportive and every weekend would drive down to Clacton to stay with Jane and discuss aspects of the recovery programme with her. I was intrigued by the Twelve Step tradition and inquired whether outsiders could attend meetings of Alcoholics Anonymous or Narcotics Anonymous. Jane explained that some were 'open' meetings to which anyone could attend and others were 'closed' meetings in which only addicts could be present.

I soon attended my first open meeting. I found the experience very positive, in marked contrast to the meeting I had attended at Godden Green. Here members, of both sexes and all ages gave accounts of their horrific experiences as addicts, but unlike the patients in the clinic, many former addicts were celebrating years of 'clean time' often running into double figures. Here was hope! The members believed that by attending regular meetings and practising the Twelve Steps they could finally free themselves of their addictive behaviour.

During these early days of recovery, Jane spent much of her time collecting stones from Clacton beach. These were not just any old stones, but tiny pieces of granite which had been rounded by constant attrition at sea. She collected only those that were coloured blue, grey or green. Rucksack by rucksack, she slowly collected and transported enough stones to cover the small area in front of her new home. I had never seen a garden like this before, the effect was stunning; the granite contained small pieces of mica which glistened when wet and sparkled like diamonds when the sun shone. Dave, Steven (her brother) and I also helped in this task. I found it very relaxing; I loved being by the sea and could understand why Jane spent so much of her time on the beach; it was very therapeutic and gave her a focus to occupy time when she was not attending meetings.

On one stone collecting trip, Jane, Steven and Dave were busily filling their rucksacks when they were approached by two booted and suited officials from Tendring District Council. The taller and more aggressive looking of the two men spoke first, 'What exactly do you think you are doing?' he said in an authoritative voice.

'Collecting stones!' stated Steven, not in the least bit intimidated by anyone in authority.

'Well, you can tip them all out, right now!' ordered the second official.

'Why?' chorused Jane and Steven in unison.

The taller man was becoming very annoyed at their lack of deference and decided to increase the pressure: 'Because if you don't, we will call the police!'

'And what will they do?' asked Steven. 'What law are we breaking?'

The smaller of the councillors seemed determined to get involved in the dispute. 'You are endangering the sea defences!' he stated, as though this master trump card settled the issue. If this is what he really thought, he had sadly miscalculated the effect of his contribution.

Jane, Steven and Dave burst into spontaneous laughter!

Dave had been a practising lawyer before he became addicted to facial surgery and was thoroughly enjoying the spectacle of the two councillors making fools of themselves in front of the gathering crowd of tourists who were curious to find out what was going on. In his quiet measured tone of voice, he said: 'I think you will find that the beach belongs to Her Majesty the Queen of England, not to Tendring District Council. As for endangering the sea defences by removing these small stones, that is a ridiculous suggestion! The beach will be far better for the children to play on with the stones removed.'

The two councillors were speechless. Finally, the taller one broke the silence. 'How do you know who owns the beach? You're not a lawyer!'

'Oh, but I am!' said Dave. 'However, I will talk to my two friends about your request.' He pronounced the word 'request' in such a way as to suggest that the councillors were overstepping their authority by ordering the removal of the stones from their rucksacks. The faces of the two officials became red with embarrassment.

Dave, Steven and Jane formed a private huddle to discuss the situation. Dave suggested that they should defer to the councillors' request because, although he had acted confidently, he was not one hundred percent certain of the legal position. Later on at night they could always revisit the spot to collect the stones after the councillors had finished work for the day.

Steven reluctantly agreed to Dave's suggestion, but inwardly would have preferred to thwart the councillors to see if they really would summon the police!

Having reached their decision, Dave acted as spokesperson for the three of them.

'On this occasion, to save you from further embarrassment, we will replace the stones we have collected.'

They slowly and carefully tipped the contents of their half-filled bags back onto the sand, making sure that their mounds were well beyond the reach of the incoming tide, finally kicking the mounds to scatter the stones over a small area.

The officials were duly satisfied and returned to their chauffeur-driven car to be taken back to the Council Chambers.

In January of the New Year, Dave booked himself into an American clinic in Boston to undergo more facial surgery. He was finding it increasingly difficult to persuade UK doctors to carry out further cosmetic work, as they were becoming aware of dysmorphobia and were under pressure from the BMA to fully investigate any client applying for such surgery. The code governing such treatment in USA was less stringent and several doctors were offering this service. Realising that the facial operation would impair his vision for a while, Dave very generously offered to pay for Jane to fly to Boston with him and help him through his recovery period. She gratefully accepted the chance to visit America, realising that while she was there assisting Dave she would be able to attend some AA and NA meetings.

During the three week stay, Jane managed to attend a dozen or so meetings and attend the Annual Boston AA convention which was even more helpful to her recovery. It was after one of the talks in a closed room that she was introduced to 'Top Cop', the future father of her son.

Top Cop worked for the Metropolitan Police based at Scotland

Yard; hence his nick-name. He was a former alcoholic but had been clean for eleven years. He was a friendly guy and offered to meet Jane in London and take her to some meetings. Jane really needed support at this time and thought this was an ideal opportunity to attend meetings with a trustworthy escort. She would feel safe and secure in the company of a policeman.

On her return to the UK, Jane rang Top Cop and arranged to meet him in London to attend a meeting of N.A. During the following weeks and months they attended many meetings and Jane's recovery continued to flourish, although her 'Step' work with her sponsor, Farmer Tony, was not making the same progress.

The months flashed by and Jane was soon celebrating one year's clean time at her home meeting place in Clacton. In December, Top Cop very generously offered to pay for Jane to accompany him on his annual visit to the Boston AA convention. She was reluctant to accept this offer for fear it might make her feel obligated to him, but it seemed too good a chance to turn down. She decided to ask me what I felt about the issue.

I suggested an alternative. 'Why not spend Christmas in Canada with me? We can stay at Sylvia and Ivan's house in Brampton and then you can fly to Boston in the New Year. I'll pay for all your flights and that way you will be under no obligation to Top Cop.' Jane jumped at the idea. 'That's very kind,' she said. 'Are you sure you want to spend all that money on me?'

I did not reply, but the look on my face told her all she needed to know.

Christmas in Brampton was cold with temperatures of minus 20 degrees Centigrade on several days. The drive leading to Sylvia's house had to be cleared of snow each morning before Ivan could extricate his car from the night's seasonal downfall and set off for work at the airport. Jane and I enjoyed assisting with this task as it proved quite exhilarating working in the freezing cold and then returning indoors to the warm, centrally heated house for a cup of piping hot chocolate.

The holiday passed all too quickly and before we had a chance to settle into any kind of routine, Jane and I were on our way back to Toronto Pearson Airport to continue with our respective journeys: Jane flying to Boston USA and me flying to Heathrow, London. It was during her visit to the AA convention in Boston that Jane became pregnant by Top Cop.

Chapter Twenty-Six: Devastating News!

When I learned of Jane's pregnancy, I was saddened: I wished I had been the father. Once I had accepted the situation, I tried to adopt a more positive attitude. I recalled that when Jane was nineteen years old she had been hospitalised for several days with cysts on her uterus. The doctor treating her had warned of the possible consequences of removing the cysts, citing an inability to bear children as the most likely serious side affect. Consequently, Jane was convinced that she would be unable to have children. This hadn't concerned her a great deal, because after her traumatic sexual abuse as a child, she was adamant that she did not want to have any children.

On my next visit to Clacton, Jane asked my views on the pregnancy. Should she have an abortion or should she have the child?

Before I gave my answer, I inquired about her feelings towards Top Cop. I was expecting Jane to admit that she had fallen head over heels in love with him. I was completely taken aback by her answer.

'I don't even like the guy!' she said.

'So, why on earth did you sleep with him?' I quizzed her, more fiercely than I intended.

'A sense of obligation, I suppose.'

I was totally perplexed as to why Jane would want to sleep with a man she did not like. *Women are so illogical!*

'OK, let's get back to the question you asked; I think you should have the child. The doctors at the Pilgrim Hospital thought you might be unable to have children, so this pregnancy is a bonus. I am sure Top Cop will be delighted to become a father and will support you financially. As for me, I look forward to helping you bring up the child. I'm sure you know that whatever decision you make, I will support it all the way.'

Jane had already reached her decision by a slightly different route. She did not fancy having an abortion and carrying a child would give her a huge incentive to stay clean: it would become the focal point of her life. My offer of support was the icing on the cake; she knew she would need all the help she could get.

'Honestly, I don't know if I'll have the patience to bring up a child,' she admitted.

'I have every confidence that you will be a superb mother,' I stated putting my arms around her and giving her a hug.

The pregnancy proceeded without any undue problems and Jane spent all of her time reorganising the cottage in preparation for the arrival of the baby. She decided that the small spare room would become the baby's room; so this was where the cot and changing top were installed. Being a perfectionist, Jane insisted on redecorating the entire cottage! The dark brown coloured woodwork was repainted with silver paint and all the walls were covered in light pastel shades of green and cream. The cheap carpet which was laid on all the floors was already badly stained and she employed a local handyman, called Graham to rip this up and replace it with interlocking wooden flooring. All this renovation was finally finished just before the birth of her child.

The end of July brought mixed emotional feelings for me. I had been invited to drive part-way across Canada, from Toronto to Vancouver, to help nephew Ken transport some of his belongings to his new residence in Duncan on Vancouver Island.

Ken planned to use his 4x4 truck to tow a trailer on which would be his powerful Yamaha FZ1 motor bike. Ken used this bike for racing on circuits in Atlanta, USA, but he had added a few extras to make it roadworthy for driving on public highways.

He had decided to drive the first 2,000 miles or so almost non-stop and then break the journey for a few days once he reached the Rockies. Here he would spend a few nights in motels. This proposition really appealed to me as I loved driving and the opportunity to ride pillion on Ken's bike with the towering, enchanting Rockies as a backdrop was too exciting to miss. But, on the other hand, I was fearful of what might happen to Jane whilst I was away. I did not trust Graham one little bit. I managed to assuage my deepest worries by promising to contact Jane every day to obtain reports on her situation.

The schedule was for me to arrive in Brampton a few days before Ken. This would give me a chance to spend some quality time with my sister and brother-in-law before Ken drove up from Atlanta and we set off on our epic three thousand mile journey across the breadth of Canada. Everything went according to schedule with Ken arriving in Brampton three days after me.

We did not leave for Vancouver immediately, as Ken wanted to unwind and relax after his long drive from Atlanta. He decided to make one overnight stay at Brampton, using the time to look up a former girl friend who lived just outside the city limits. Rather than use the 4x4 with its trailer to negotiate the busy urban roads, Ken unloaded his Yamaha FZ1 motor bike, donned his leathers and set off, winding his way out of the estate at high speed. I could tell from the noise coming from Ken's bike engine that this was a highly tuned machine!

On his return, Ken offered to take me for a spin on the bike. I loved the exhilaration of riding pillion at high speed, especially when the driver was as competent as Ken. After I struggled into the tight fitting spare set of leathers that Ken provided, I fastened my crash helmet and I was eager to set off.

We headed westwards out of the estate towards the highway. The roads were busy but the acceleration of the bike was phenomenal and we rapidly wove our way in and out of the traffic until we reached the highway. Once on the dual carriageway Ken unleashed the full power of the bike. It was not only the top speed which was awesome but the rate of acceleration and deceleration; one minute we were travelling at 120mph the next we throttled down to a mere 30mph as thirty-two wheeled rigs blocked both lanes. To me we only seemed to be on the bike for a few minutes before we were back at Sylvia and Ivan's house; in reality, we had been riding for over an hour! I loved every minute of it and couldn't wait to arrive in the Rockies! When I asked Ken about our top speed, Ken nonchalantly stated that we had reached over

130mph when overtaking the white, Dodge Viper two seated sports car!

Ken and I were night men, both preferring the late evening hours rather than the early morning ones. Therefore, the next day we made a leisurely mid-morning departure after devouring a large breakfast of cereals, eggs, toast, fruit and several cups of coffee.

Ken had previously travelled across Canada on the Trans Canadian Highway and found the Prairies flat and rather uninteresting, so he suggested that for the first part of our journey we should each drive for three hour spells, only stopping for food and toilets. I readily agreed to this plan as I was accustomed to covering over 750 miles, in one day, on the crowded UK roads. Driving on the comparatively deserted Canadian highways would be a breeze, even with the trailer.

Ken took the first turn at the wheel. Having lived and worked in Toronto several years ago, he still remembered his way around the city.

We initially headed north to Georgian Bay then north-west to Sudbury. This part of the journey was slow as we encountered a lot of heavy traffic. Ken completed his three-hour stint and I took over. The hours passed quickly and the miles raced by.

After we had both driven for several three-hour shifts, at around 2.00am in the morning I found myself heading towards the town of Sault Sainte Marie. On the opposite side of the road, I noticed what appeared to be an abandoned car. Travelling at over 90mph I had little chance to fully observe if there were any occupants in the car as I flashed by, but instinct warned me that it might be an unmarked police car and I slowed down to a more respectable 70mph. Sure enough, within seconds, I heard the unmistakable wailing sound of a police siren! I further slowed the truck to the legal 60mph limit, but by now the police car had almost caught up with us and was flashing its lights to tell us to stop. I woke Ken from his deep slumber.

A rather large officer was soon standing at the side of the driver's window demanding to see my driving licence and Ken's ownership and insurance documents. As soon as these were handed over he disappeared from sight, walking back to his car to process the information. It seemed an eternity before he returned, but this was no bad thing as it gave Ken time to become more alert.

What the officer said next is forever etched in my memory!

'You boys are driving far too fast! The moose round here are mighty big and if you hit one at the speed you were travelling you would not survive!' The officer continued. 'If I booked you at the speed you were going, it would cost you a $350 fine, but I have reduced this to $146. You can pay by cash or credit card at our local office. Now drive more carefully boys and keep your speed down!'

Having delivered this warning the officer turned and disappeared into the night. Taking his advice, I resumed the journey at a more leisurely pace. Almost immediately Ken fell back to sleep and dark isolation enveloped our truck once again.

By daybreak we reached Thunder Bay and made a 'pit stop' for fuel, breakfast and toilets. Over a steaming cup of hot coffee we discussed the night's misadventure. I used Ken's mobile to contact the Sault Sainte Marie office to pay the speeding fine. I was surprised to learn that the fine could not be paid over the phone: credit cards could only be used manually at their office. As we were now over five hundred miles from the town, this was impossible. A cheque could be sent by post, but Ken did not have his cheque book with him. Therefore, I decided to leave the issue until my return to the UK.

Once out of Thunder Bay there was little traffic on the Highway. We were soon leaving Ontario and driving into Manitoba. The milometer recorded our speedy progress through the flat prairie lands. The scenery had a monotonous similarity to it and I was disappointed that I saw very little wildlife. Nonetheless, I found the driving quite exhilarating.

By 6.00pm we were within range of Regina, in Saskatchewan and Ken suggested this would be a good place to make an overnight stop to catch up on some 'proper' sleep!

Most of the motels we drove past on the outskirts of the town were already displaying 'No vacancy' signs and it soon became clear that finding reasonably priced accommodation might be more difficult than we had imagined. Finally, we resorted to exploring side streets rather than the main 'drag' and drove past several hotels with vacancies.

We chose one for its name rather than any other quality, as it was impossible to gauge the standard of their accommodation from the outside. The Regina Regency Motel sounded sufficiently imposing to warrant further investigation and having parked our truck outside the reception office we walked wearily into the entrance to speak to the young girl at the desk.

She was bright and alert. 'We do have a few rooms left but they are all on the smoking corridor.' As both of us were ardent non-smokers, this did not seem a very attractive proposition. However, the thought of more driving was even less appealing, so we reluctantly agreed to accept. We were offered room 28 and were assured that the last occupants had been light smokers and the room did not smell too badly of stale tobacco!

Ken and I had agreed to go halves on all expenses, so I produced a credit card from my wallet to settle the night's accommodation. Having secured the room, we returned to the truck to unload our travelling cases.

Room 28 was spacious with two king sized beds. I threw my case onto the bed and shot into the washroom, whilst Ken returned to the truck to collect his bike leathers, informing me they were far too valuable to leave on display in the truck. On his return Ken was very animated! 'Grab your stuff Paul! We've been given a non-smoking room!'

We hastily collected our belongings and descended a floor, to room 11. After unpacking only a few essential items, we made a spontaneous decision to go into the town for something to eat. I glanced round for my wallet, but it was nowhere to be seen. Ken, impatient to be on his way, asked what was causing the delay. As soon as I informed him of the missing wallet, Ken was all support. 'OK,' he said, 'I'll go and check in the truck. You look in your case!'

After five minutes Ken returned empty handed. 'Have you had any luck?' The question was rhetorical as the grim expression on my face gave the answer.

'Let's apply a little logic to the situation,' suggested Ken. 'When can you remember last seeing it?'

I focused my thoughts! 'When I paid the receptionist for the room,' I stated confidently, detailed memories flooding back into my conscious mind. 'So I must have left the wallet in your truck, or in room 28.'

We raced down to reception. The young receptionist, ever eager to please, informed us that a couple had already taken the room we had recently vacated so she would ring and ask them to look for the wallet. Ken and I could barely contain our anxiety as we listened to the receptionist's request for a thorough search of the room for the wallet. After several minutes of deafening silence we were told that nothing had been found.

On returning to our room, Ken insisted that I mentally retrace my steps once again. Within a matter of seconds, I could clearly see myself placing the wallet on top of the television in room 28. This I told Ken, who without ever questioning anything, jumped into action. 'Follow me!' he instructed as he raced out of the room, up the stairs, along the corridor to room 28. Positioned in the centre of the door, Ken drew himself to his full six foot two inches of height and rapped loudly on the door. A petite, attractive, young girl of about nineteen years of age partially opened the door. She seemed very nervous. Looking up at Ken's towering figure did not improve her disposition in the least! Ken spoke, his voice laden with power and authority. 'We know the wallet is in there on the television, now bring it out!' The girl retreated not completely closing the door as she went. Ken and I could hear muffled voices coming from inside. Within a short space of time the girl returned and handed my wallet over to Ken.

'Check the money!' Ken commanded.

Much to my relief, it was all there! I had no idea what Ken would have done had some been missing! Over the intervening years, I have never forgotten this incident and continually marvel at Ken's complete faith in my memory and the powerful command he exerted over the dishonest couple who must have planned to steal the wallet.

Before leaving the following morning Ken and I accrued some good karma by helping a middle-aged American lady to start her car with Ken's jump leads. Ken refused her repeated offer of money, but did agree to let her buy us a coffee at the local restaurant.

After another hard day's driving, we arrived at the Rockies, where Ken had planned a two day sabbatical from the rigours of the road. At Banff we found a delightful motel complete with sauna, heated indoor swimming pool and a majestic snow-covered mountain backdrop. As soon as we had checked in and transported our belongings into the room, Ken was keen to unload the Yamaha, don his leathers and go for a spin. I was equally enthusiastic to view the breathtaking scenery from the pillion seat of the bike!

We cruised slowly and carefully through the small town before rejoining the Trans-Canadian Highway. Once on the open road, Ken fully opened the throttle and we raced through the mountain passes with their massive, snow-covered peaks on either side. Ken drove for about half an hour before turning round and heading back to Banff. Back in the motel we crashed onto our individual king-sized beds to relax our weary limbs. I asked Ken if I could borrow his mobile phone to give Jane a quick ring to find out if everything was OK with her.

I constantly marvel at modern technology: the ability to converse with someone over four thousand miles away never ceases to amaze me. Jane's voice was as clear as a bell. Yes, she was fine, but had just missed the ferry to Ireland and would have to wait several hours for the next one. I immediately sensed that something was wrong. Jane always allowed plenty of spare time when planning such excursions. Unless her car had broken down or an accident had blocked one of the roads on her route she would not have missed the ferry. I started to delve further by asking a series of questions. Jane faltered and finally broke down.

'Graham raped me this morning before I left. I didn't want to tell you until you arrived back because I knew it would ruin your holiday.'

I was speechless; tears streamed down my face. I made no effort to hide the tears from Ken. 'Have you reported it to the police?'

'Not yet, I just wanted to get to Ireland to see Liz.'

I was so emotional I could not think clearly. I needed time to come to terms with the appalling news. Finally, after remaining silent for what seemed like an eternity, I told Jane to ring me, whatever time of day or night, on this mobile from Liz's home phone.

Ken, intuitive by nature, had already grasped the seriousness of the situation and was sitting bolt upright on the bed. 'What has happened Paul?' he asked with tenderness.

My answer was explicit: 'Jane's been raped!'

It was Ken's turn to be shell-shocked.

I spent the next half hour briefing Ken on background information about Graham the decorator and events prior to the rape. Ken was totally supportive. 'I would go back to the UK immediately if I were you. If you want me to sort this bloke out, I am more than happy to fly over to the UK and put him in a wheel chair for the rest of his life!'

Having seen Ken's positive, authoritative handling of the situation with the 'stolen' wallet, I had no doubt that Ken would be as good as his word! Having such a solid, reliable friend helped ease my troubled mind, but I continued to remain tearful and emotional. Two unanswered questions kept occupying my mind – would the unborn child be damaged by the rape and would the rape cause Jane to relapse in her recovery?

After considering all the possible options, I decided that I would try and return to the UK on an earlier flight than booked, but would not leave Canada until Jane had returned to the UK from Ireland. Further decisions could be made once she had spoken to me on Liz's phone.

Within a few hours Jane rang from Glendalough and I learned

of the morning's tragic events. Graham had rung Jane from his mobile at 7.00am. Jane seeing that it was Graham on the phone did not answer. A short while later, he turned up outside the front door and rang the doorbell. Half asleep, Jane went to the door, saw that it was Graham and asked what he wanted. He informed her that he had accidentally left, in her home, some of his paintbrushes which he needed that morning for a new job he was starting. Nervously, she opened the door. As she did so her alarm went off in the bedroom: the wake-up call to prepare for her departure to Ireland. She went to turn it off. Graham followed her into the bedroom, grabbed her from behind, pushed her on to the bed and raped her. With his massive six foot plus frame and weighing over sixteen stone, Jane had no chance to fight him off.

The devastating news left me numb with shock and horror. Later, I could not recall anything I had said to Jane other than making her promise to report the rape to the police on her return to the UK.

True to her promise, Jane reported the rape to the Clacton-on-Sea Police on her return from Ireland and investigations were started in mid-August. On December 25th 2005 Graham Swan was arrested and charged with raping Jane Gray.

Chapter Twenty-Seven: The Rape Trial

The court case took place at Chelmsford Crown Court on Monday 17th July 2006. I kept my own diary of the case, although I was not allowed in the courtroom until I had given my evidence in the witness box, so I missed some parts of the case including Jane and Liz's evidence. But, despite missing vital parts of the case, I learnt much about the UK's criminal law system[1].

One of the crucial facts I learnt was that the accused seems to have all the advantages. Although Jane and I had asked to see the Crown Prosecuting Barrister before the case began, this request was denied and we met Mr Thompson, for the first time, ten minutes before the case started. Graham Swan, on the other hand, had the distinct advantage of working with Miss Kate Davey, his Defending Barrister, throughout the weeks prior to the trial, carefully planning to exploit the weak points in Jane's allegations.

During the trial before the Judge, the Honourable David Turner QC, the Prosecution presented their evidence first and then the Defence had a chance to reply. In the summing up, once again the Prosecution went first, followed by the Defence. It soon became clear to me that the latter evidence was more likely to be remembered and make an impression on the Jury than the earlier evidence.

This became all too clear when the Jury had retired to consider their verdict and asked for a transcript of Jane's evidence on day one of the trial! Their request was denied and they had to rely on any fleeting memories that might remain in their minds after so many differing statements had been made; but it proved to Liz and me that by day four, the members of the Jury could remember little of the earlier evidence and that it was the most recent statements that would make the deepest impression!

---

1 For those readers who enjoy following court proceedings, a transcript of the hearing can be obtained from Her Majesty's Government Records

Grudgingly, I have to admit that Miss Kate Davey, Counsel for the Defence, was excellent. In her summing up she repeatedly told the Jury that she did not have to prove Graham Swan's innocence, but if the Jury had even the slightest doubt about his guilt they must acquit him.

The Honourable David Turner QC had the final words. He summarised the arguments of both sides in the case, suggesting to the Jury that they should consider each piece of evidence on merit and decide which witnesses they felt were trustworthy. He repeated Miss Davey's caution, that they should only convict Graham Swan if they had no doubts as to his guilt. With this final piece of advice ringing in their ears, the Jury retired to their room to deliberate on their verdict.

We waited nervously for over two hours. Twice during this time, everyone involved in the case was summoned into the courtroom. On both occasions the Foreman of the Jury was seeking clarification on minor legal points. Finally the tannoy summoned everyone connected with the case 'Regina versus Swan' to Court Four for the third and last time.

The Jury filed back into the room and seated themselves, apart for the Foreman who remained standing facing the Judge.

'Have you reached a verdict?' asked the Right Honourable David Turner QC.

'Yes, we have reached a majority verdict,' replied the Foreman in a solemn tone of voice. 'Not guilty!'

After this devastating court verdict I realised that the next few weeks would be crucially important for Jane's future. I was also deeply affected by the verdict. After all, I had persuaded Jane to bring the rape charge against Graham Swan. How, I pondered, could twelve members of the public reach such a wrong verdict?

It was only later when Ken and I carried out some Internet research that we discovered that the conviction rate for rape in the UK is appallingly low; very few reported cases ever get to court and those that do have a 15% conviction rate!

From this experience I would advise anyone seeking redress through the UK courts to think very carefully before initiating any proceedings! Hiring lawyers and barristers is a very expensive business and the court itself is like a giant theatre of expectations. Frequently, it appears, the outcome of the case is decided not on justice, but on which side has the best legal representation. This viewpoint was confirmed by the verdict in Jane's rape case and later in my own legal efforts to enforce my Contact Order with James Gray.

Chapter Twenty-Eight: The Birth of James

Fortunately for all concerned, the rape ordeal did not visibly affect Jane's pregnancy. However, she was very fearful of being on her own in the cottage at night, but her many friends rallied round to keep her company during this difficult time.

I travelled down to Clacton at every opportunity. I was now on a part-time teaching contract, working only the first three days of each week, so every Wednesday evening, after arriving home from school, I would change into casual clothes, pack a few essentials for the weekend's stay and race down to Clacton. It was during one of these visits at the end of September that James was born. It was a day I will never forget!

On Friday 30th September 2005 I was staying in Clacton. I awoke at 7.15am when Jane brought me a cup of tea. She explained that she had not slept much all night and was struggling to move properly. 'It's going to be a real snail day!' she said jokingly. Shortly afterwards Jane's contractions started and she slowly walked around the cottage preparing her hospital bag for herself and the eagerly awaited arrival.

We were soon on our journey to Colchester General Hospital with me at the wheel of my red Toyota Corolla. The atmosphere was relaxed and calm even though it was rush hour with heavy traffic. We chatted during the drive. All was well with the world! D Day had finally arrived!

The birth was not easy. Jane went into labour at 2.00pm, but James did not make an appearance until 8.25pm and even then had to be enticed out by suction! Everyone involved in the birth was exhausted, except Jane who seemed to be in a remarkably cheerful state considering all that she had been through. She even asked the midwife if she could have a shower and some food!

Once Jane had been stitched and cleansed, she and I went down to the special care room to look at James. He was in a small glass cradle and was sound asleep. He had a blue woollen hat on his head and looked very peaceful.

Whilst convalescing in hospital Jane started to write an account of the birth of her son and asked me if I would contribute to this. I was only too happy to oblige as I felt honoured that Jane had requested my presence at the birth. This is what I wrote:

"Looking back on the day's experience, it was one of the most moving days of my life. Birth and death are at the opposite ends of the scale, but during both of them you seem to be very close to the Creator. Whether you are a spiritual person or not, I cannot believe that anyone could witness the birth of a child without being profoundly moved by the whole experience. It was a privilege to be there and I will always be grateful to Jane for allowing me to be present at such a wonderfully special occasion."

Jane was not allowed home the following day; in fact it was several days before she was discharged and allowed to return to Pickle Cottage with James her son. Jane herself had come through the ordeal of birth remarkably well, but James was kept under observation because the sleeping tablets which Jane was taking prior to his birth had caused him to be rather shaky and he slept more than was customary for a newborn baby. But soon all the hospital's concerns vanished and I was delighted to be transporting the couple home.

Peter, one of her friends from the Clacton N.A. group, had prepared a warm homecoming, hanging a large banner embossed with the words, 'Welcome Home' across the front windows of the cottage!

From day one, I immersed myself in the exhausting but immensely rewarding task of helping Jane to raise her son. Certainly the all-consuming task of caring for James was very therapeutic for Jane and it was fortunate that she had no opportunity to dwell on the implications of Graham Swan's acquittal.

The decision to have the child provided her salvation and it was a decision she would never regret, for the birth of her son brought untold happiness and fulfilment which in some small measure compensated for all the terrible ordeals of her childhood. For me it was another story!

Part Two:
James Gray

Chapter One: James' early years

Every weekend I travelled down to Clacton to help Jane look after James and soon became very attached to the youngster. When he was four months old, Jane asked me if I would take him to Boston for a few days to give her a break from the constant pressure of bringing up a baby. I was only too happy to oblige, so James made his first visit to Boston when he was a few months old.

He was a very easy child to look after as he rarely cried and was seldom sick. The original plan had been for James to stay in Boston for about five days, but after two days had elapsed Jane was already missing him terribly and asked me to bring him back to Clacton.

On my visits to Clacton, I would take James for long walks - at the beginning in his pram and later in his pushchair. Whatever the weather (rain, sleet, or snow) I could be seen pushing James along the seafront! As he became older and more alert, I would take some cheese with me to feed the seagulls. James loved this and became very animated by the close proximity of these noisy sea birds.

Once his personality started to develop, his infectious smile was irresistible and everyone fell in love with the handsome baby. I gave him the nickname 'Chuckleberry', because he was always laughing and smiling. I frequently heard him chuckling whilst asleep, as though he was having a marvellous dream and he always awoke in the morning with a smile on his face.

According to Jane, he was slow to learn to talk and at one stage she considered referring him to a speech therapist to see if there were any underlying problems preventing him from talking. She need not have worried. Once he started to talk, his language development was nothing short of phenomenal! He not only came out with some incredibly complicated words and sentences but he understood what they meant!

He soon started to call me 'Pookie', a family nickname for me. I was quite happy to respond to this as it saved confusion between the two Pauls (his father also being called Paul). James had a great sense of humour and loved to get up to 'his trickeries' as he called them. Others may have labelled such activities as mischief!

He was naturally funny and came out with some priceless sayings. I vividly remembered standing on the balcony at Clacton Leisure Centre, watching James play five-a-side football. James was four and a half years old at the time, but Jane had told the football coach that he was five, as this was the minimum age for enrolment in this course!

James was very fit for his age and had been running non-stop for about ten minutes when he came to a complete standstill in the middle of the pitch. Adam, the coach went up to him and asked, 'What's the problem James?'

James shrugged his shoulders. 'I've run out of fuel and my engine is overheating!'

All the parents started to laugh, not just because it was funny, but also because of the serious way in which he said it.

I also started to teach him to play badminton, although hitting the shuttle proved rather difficult for James. He always persevered, knowing that this was my favourite sport. James' greatest achievement was on the trampoline. He had a natural aptitude for this sport and would spend hours at a time bouncing high into the air. He literally had to be dragged away when it was time to leave!

Like all children, James loved playing games. Because he was so well travelled he had rapidly learnt the names of all the main airports in the UK and would spend hours on end taking off and landing his planes at the various imaginary airports. He would become totally absorbed in these activities. Getting him to bed at a reasonable time became increasing difficult!

I loved spending time with James and knowing how much he enjoyed splashing in water, I regularly took him to the Colchester Aqua Springs pool. James took to water like a duck and was very daring, jumping into the water from the side and travelling down the slides at great speed. His love of water was nearly his undoing when on holiday in Victoria, Canada.

Delphine and Stuart had a Border Collie called Scotia and James had been throwing sticks into the river for him to fetch, when he decided to jump into the river himself! Jane was the first to react and threw her expensive camera onto the bank before managing to pull him out of the water. The camera slid into the river, a small price to pay for the rescue of her son! James seemed none the worst for the experience and the next day was jumping into the water at the local swimming pool with his usual bravado!

When we visited Clacton beach James would spend hour after hour playing with his sand toys. These consisted of a bucket and spade, a medium-sized cement mixer, a couple of small trucks and a very large tipper truck. He delighted in building castles with moats which he filled with water. He always built at least two settlements, many metres apart and he would race his tipper truck from one settlement to the other carrying 'cement' which he made by mixing sand, water and gravel together.

From our frequent visits to the swimming pool, I knew that James loved being in the water; on one of our visits to the beach I purchased a plastic dinghy. This proved to be a tremendous hit with James. We would paddle out to the buoy which was situated about four hundred metres from the shore and pretend to be rescuing stranded tourists who had been trapped when the tide came in.

A charming incident occurred when James was four years old. Jane and I were shopping at the ASDA supermarket in Boston when James disappeared. We checked throughout the store but couldn't find him. We asked the security guard if he had seen a young child leaving the store. His answer was 'No!' We were about to call the police to report a missing child, when James walked in through the entrance doors.

When I asked him where he had been he told me that he had bought himself a lorry and taken it to the 'Red Rocket' to put it on the back seat. When I rebuked him for taking it without paying he was most upset!

'But I did pay for it Pookie!'

'How?' I asked. 'You have no money!'

'I scanned it through the till!' he proudly replied.

Sure enough there was video evidence of James scanning the lorry on the store's self-pay tills!

This incident was recorded in my evidence at Chelmsford County Court. It shows his adult behaviour at such a young age. I never ceased to be amazed by James. He was a delightful and unusual child. The bond between us grew ever stronger.

Chapter Two: Contact denied!

On my week-end visits to Clacton, I would spend most of my time with James because I enjoyed his company so much. Until James reached the age of four, Jane seemed quite happy with this arrangement as it gave her a chance to unwind and relax without the responsibility of watching over a very active young boy.

However, I was unaware that Jane was feeling ignored and failed to see the consequences of this. James was the focus of my attention. Jane was slipping into the background where she began to look outside of our little circle for friendship and social contacts. In my adoration of her son, I was unable to see what was happening to the mother. Then Jane dropped her bombshell! It came as a total surprise and my world fell apart!

In May 2009 Jane informed me that I was no longer welcome down in Clacton as she had a new boyfriend and wanted to make a fresh start. She warned me that if I ignored her request to stay away from them, I would have to answer to her new boyfriend and he could turn nasty! To make matters worse, she told me that from now on I would not be allowed to see her son James.

I was devastated: it was as though my heart had been ripped out! I was to be denied contact with the most important person in my life! Why, oh why, was Jane acting in this way after all I had done for her and her son, James?

I decided to do all within my power to persuade Jane to change her mind. However, whenever I rang Jane, Richard would answer the phone and refuse to let me talk to her. His tone was aggressive and he threatened me with dire consequences if I persisted in trying to contact her.

Undeterred, I wrote to Jane and my letter persuaded her to meet me in Clacton. I can vividly remember the details of this visit and on my return to Boston wrote down exactly what had happened:

I arrived first. As I approached the agreed rendezvous, the aroma of freshly ground coffee wafted into my nostrils. I peered inside the café, but the small interior was dimly lit and crowded with noisy customers taking a break from their Friday shopping.

I decided to sit outside on a white, uncomfortable plastic chair, with a matching plastic table in front of me. At least the sun was shining and its warm rays invigorated me. I placed a one pound punnet of freshly picked strawberries in the centre of the table. This drew admiring glances from several passers-by, one even offering to purchase it!

Jane, and her brother Steven, joined me five minutes later and sat on the opposite side of the table. All three of us ordered lattes. The atmosphere was tense and I realised that the meeting wasn't going to be easy. I inwardly winced, but said nothing. Jane broke the silence.

'I've read your letter.'

'So, can I see James?' I replied eagerly.

'No!'

'Why not?'

'Because I don't want to jeopardise my relationship with Richard.'

'But, you promised I could see James!'

'Look Paul, no disrespect,' butted in Steven, 'but Jane is with Richard now and wants you out of her life. In my opinion you have been far too involved with her in the past.'

I winced again. Steven knew nothing of our long, tumultuous relationship that stretched back over many years. I remained silent as Steven droned on. Jane occasionally interjected with comments about my lack of discipline with James and how her son had once climbed on to the roof of the 'Red Rocket' - James's name for my battered old Toyota Corolla which had recently clocked up 250,000 miles - and, how I hadn't told him off!

I continued to remain silent, although I was severely tempted to end this two-pronged verbal attack and declare war on Jane. I knew in my heart that war was inevitable as I had tried every persuasive ploy at my disposal, but all had failed miserably!

Jane's 'No! No! No!' echoed through my mind. I decided to make one last effort to bring about a change of heart.

'Steven, I need to speak to Jane alone.'

'Why?'

'Because I do!' I spoke these words emphatically enough to prevent further discussion.

Steven reluctantly accepted the situation and stood up.

'OK, I'll go to my bank and be back in ten minutes. Will you be all right, Sis?'

'Yes.'

Steven shuffled off, head down, texting someone on his mobile as he left.

At last, I thought, I can express my true feelings about the situation. However, before I could say a word, Jane burst into tears.

'You know I don't want to stop you seeing James.'

Jane's reaction and words took me by surprise.

'So why on earth are you stopping me?'

'Things have changed. Ever since you told Richard that you loved me, he has become paranoid about me having any contact with you. If I allow you to see James, I will have to negotiate with you and Richard will not agree to that, so it's not going to happen.'

'But Jane you promised, many times, that I could see James and Richard should not prevent you from keeping your promise. So, when can I see him?'

Jane's face lost its soft, sympathetic look and a mask of hard, cold logic replaced it. My despair was increasing by the minute. I realised that any form of compromise would be well-nigh impossible.

Despite the sinking feeling in my stomach, I made one last effort to persuade Jane to change her mind.

'Jane, look into my eyes!'

I paused to give her time to notice my imploring expression.

'What do you see? Hatred? Anger? No, love! Jane, I think you are an honourable person and keeping your promise is an

154

important part of behaving honourably. So, please tell me when I can see James?'

'Not at present. You must wait!'

I could not prevent a sarcastic tone creeping into my voice. 'How long? A week, a month, a year?'

Before Jane could reply, Steven returned and the conversation about James ceased. My sullen silence pervaded the atmosphere like an impending catastrophe.

Jane changed topics. 'Have you brought me the money you promised?' The word 'promised' rankled with me and I considered telling her I had no intention of giving her any money. Why should I act honourably when she was acting so dishonourably?

'Yes, but I'll have to go to the HSBC bank and draw the money out.'

I stood up, handed the punnet of strawberries to Jane and went inside to pay the waitress for the three coffees. A few minutes later I joined the others outside and all three of us strolled round the corner to the nearest branch of my bank. Jane went inside with me and Steven remained outside rolling a cigarette. There was a small queue waiting for the next available teller.

'Jane, come to James' Nursery School with me and let me see him!'

'No!'

'Then give me permission to see James at his school!'

'No!'

I felt like Moses trying to persuade Pharaoh to let the Israelites return to their homeland. Like Pharaoh, Jane refused and remained heartless.

Jane sensed my desperation and turned to face me.

'Look!' she said, catching my eyes. 'I can't stop you going to the Nursery to see him, can I?'

'No, you can't, but have you told the staff not to let me see him?'

'Of course not!'

My turn at the counter had arrived and I duly drew out £1,500 in twenty pound notes which the teller sealed in a brown

155

envelope. This was Jane's money for emergencies, which she had asked me to keep. I handed this to Jane and we walked outside to join Steven who was puffing on his roll-up. I said my goodbyes and headed off to the car park where I had left the Red Rocket. I was soon racing towards the Willows Nursery on the outskirts of Clacton. Better get there before Richard finds out and tries to stop me, I thought.

My head was filled with very mixed emotions. On the one hand, I was excited at the prospect of seeing James for the first time in over two months, but on the other hand I was filled with sadness at the thought that this might be the last time I would have contact with him for many years.

I rang the doorbell and spoke to the Secretary.

'I've come to see James Gray.'

'OK. Come in.'

The Secretary cast her eagle eyes over me as I walked past her office. I had picked James up from the Nursery on many occasions and she instantly recognised me and gave me a nod of approval.

I opened the door to James' classroom, but no-one was there. The children were all outside in the playground. I wandered through the room containing toys, models, computers and a television amongst other things and walked through the patio door which led to the playground.

James spotted me first. I took a second or two to recognise him! He seemed much smaller than I remembered and was also more subdued and serious than in the past, but soon his characteristic infectious smile appeared and I thought how smart he looked in his grey trousers and red jumper.

The initial meeting was not at all like I had envisioned. I had expected James to come running over saying, 'Pookie! Pookie! Pookie!' But this had not happened. I was unbalanced by the change in James' behaviour and stood there not knowing what to do next.

James took the initiative, holding my hand and leading me away from the other children to sit on a bench on the edge of the playground. James climbed on to my knee.

For a while there was silence between us as I struggled to compose myself. Would I ever see James again? A tear trickled slowly down my face.

James broke the silence. 'Will you be coming to my Sports Day tomorrow, to watch me run?'

I dabbed away the tear. 'I would love to, but I can't.'

'Why?'

'Because Mummy and Richard won't allow me to.'

'Why not?'

'You'll have to ask Mummy that.'

'Yes, Mummy did tell me she had an adult row with you.'

I decided to change the topic.

'Have you seen Sam, Chloe, or Charlie Helpful lately?'

'Yes, I think Sam is staying in Boston and will come and see you tomorrow.

Possibly as a result of being an only child, James had invented three companions: Sam, Chloe and Charlie Helpful. James and I often chatted about the adventures of these three friends.

'I don't like Richard!' said James 'He came into my bedroom and told me off for using two boxes of Lego at the same time. So when he went out, I hid one box behind my big teddy.'

For the first time, since I left home, I smiled.

James went on. 'I want to come to Boston and make some flapjacks, so you and Mummy can be friends again.'

Damn these tears! I thought, as I wiped my hand across my eyes and sighed. I continued to pat James gently on his back as this action soothed my raw emotions.

We talked a while longer about Yellow Pages deliveries, strawberry picking and Emilis, James' Polish friend from Boston. I wanted to stay forever, but I knew I must leave.

'I have to go James!'

The little lad reached up and kissed me and gave me a big hug. We stood up and he led me by the hand through two classrooms and a corridor to the outside entrance.

As we waved goodbye to each other, I wondered for the second time whether I would be allowed to see James again.

The visit reminded me of the painting by William Frederick Yeames, of Bonny Prince Charles being asked: 'And when did you last see your father?' I wondered whether I would ever see James again. Even Jane's own relatives urged me to try and remain in contact with him. All of them without exception believed that I was an integral part of James' life and provided the stability, love and affection that he needed as he developed. They were not sure how much love and affection he would receive from Richard, the new boyfriend!

As I continued my drive back to Boston, I wondered how many other people were suffering the same kind of heart-break that I was? It was at this very moment that I determined to put 'pen to paper' and record all the details of my forthcoming struggle to try and remain in contact with James.

It was Dariusz, my Polish friend and masseur, who suggested contacting a solicitor to see what help I might gain through legal proceedings. He pointed out that in Poland, friends involved in a child's upbringing have certain rights, even if they are not blood relatives. I promised to explore this avenue as all else had failed dismally.

On my return to Boston, I made an appointment with Paul Davey, the top family solicitor at Roseland. I was amazed to discover that contact with James, through the courts, was a real possibility. When Paul Davey learned of all my involvement with James from his birth onwards, he guaranteed that any High Court Judge would look favourably upon such an application.

So, the die was cast! I paid my money and the application for a Contact Order was initiated. I was very sad that after all our years of friendship, Jane and I should fall out so terribly.

I spent a long time preparing the document to explain to the Judge, at Colchester County Court, why I thought my contact with James was so vital for the boy's development. This document included my presence at the birth of James, my weekend visits, the long seafront walks, James' visits to Boston, teaching him to cook flapjacks and James' formula for 'fresh fruit yoghurt', the many holidays spent together, and teaching him to swim, play football, badminton and use the trampoline.

The date for the court hearing at Colchester County Court was set for early October 2010. But before the case was to be heard, Jane rang me and backed down, agreeing to abide by the draft Contact Order prepared by Paul Davey, which stated that I would be allowed to see James once a month, for four hours, on the first Saturday of each month. The court case was vacated, but nonetheless the draft document became an official document once it was stamped by a High Court Judge at Colchester County Court. I thought this legal document would deter Jane from changing her mind in the future. How wrong can one be?

Whilst on the phone, Jane told me that she was short of money and wondered if, once the strawberry season came around, I would be interested in driving down with a trailer load of strawberries to sell to the occupants of a caravan park in Clacton? She had checked with the park office and discovered that there were over six hundred caravans on the site. She offered to help me sell the strawberries in return for half the profit.

I agreed to consider this proposition, but in the meantime I was allowed to see James on 2nd October 2010. I mistakenly believed that everything was now stabilised and I would be allowed to remain in contact with James on a regular basis.

Chapter Three: Happiness!

After 2nd October 2010, not a day went by when I did not think about James and eagerly look forward to my monthly visit to Clacton-on-Sea to spend my allotted four hours with James. The visiting day always passed like a blur of lightning. I usually picked James up from Toys R Us and spent two or more happy hours at the Aqua Springs Swimming Pool in Colchester. James just loved the pool!

The fast flowing river was James' favourite attraction and he would ride on his blue coloured float called 'Zoggs'. I would hold this about two feet under the water so James could stand on it like the king of a castle and view all the other swimmers from his lofty perch. James asked me if I did this kind of thing when I was a child. I had to admit that there were no indoor swimming pools where I lived and I didn't learn to swim until I was much older than he was.

After the physical exertion of the river, we would both relax in the heated whirlpool. If it was not too crowded, James would jump in from the steps and swim across to the other side. Another favourite activity was to get me to lie on my back, in the shallow paddling pool, pretending to be a boat. James would then run to various parts of the pool picking up imaginary cases to load onto the boat. Finally, once fully loaded, James would jump onto the boat himself and verbally manoeuvre me around the pool, always finishing near the waterfall, an area where warm water cascaded down from the Jacuzzi hot tub situated above the paddling pool.

At the end of two enjoyable hours we would dry ourselves and change before purchasing some drinks and flapjacks from the vending machines. Once our appetites were assuaged we would return to the 'Red Rocket' to dump our swimming gear and take out the plastic football.

Aqua Springs had a large area of Astro-turf with several five-a-side football pitches available for free use. I loved working with James to improve his dribbling, shooting and goal-keeping skills. Occasionally some older boys who were playing invited us to join in their competitive games. James always liked to give his side a name. This was usually 'Germany' on account of their numerous successes in the World Cup! James would run non-stop and was fearless in tackling: older boys were no barrier to his determination and fitness.

These were memorable, happy times and only too quickly the four hours passed and I had to return James to his mother and Richard at Toys R Us. On the way back to Ipswich, James would tell me how he intended to improve the interior of the Red Rocket, by ripping out the old dashboard and replacing it with a new one; he would also ask me about repairing the small hole in the passenger's front door. He planned to visit Boston in his next holiday to carry out these tasks.

In January 2011, Jane asked me if I would be prepared to look after James in Boston for ten days or so, as she wanted to visit Liz in Ireland to seek her advice on a few issues. I was overjoyed at the prospect of looking after James for an extended period of time and readily agreed to this request.

So in the third week of January, I picked James up from Ipswich and we travelled the ninety miles back to Boston. Because this was term time and I was carrying out supply work as a teacher at Boston High School, I arranged for James to attend the 'Mon-Ami' Nursery School, every day, from 8.30am until 3.00pm. However, James was not on the admission role and the placing was on a daily basis, subject to availability. On the Wednesday, there were no places available! I faced a dilemma! I did not want to turn down my Wednesday morning's supply work, as this helped finance the cost of the Mon-Ami Nursery School, so I rang the High School and asked the Headmistress if James could join me for my morning of PE lessons. The Headmistress agreed to this request and James was very excited at the prospect of being a member of my classes!

Before we set off for school at 8.30am, I gave James some last minute instructions about behaving in a sensible manner. I need not have worried; James was a model pupil. He joined in with all of the lessons. One of these was year eight football outdoors on the school's playing field. James was in his element either chasing after the ball or running round the outside of the pitch. After the lesson finished, when I blew the final whistle some of the boys threw their bibs on the ground where they were standing, rather than return them to the pile at the edge of the pitch. Without waiting for instructions, James raced round the pitch picking up all the scattered bibs and then carried them all into the pavilion where the boys were changing.

The year seven girls had a lesson of badminton in the gymnasium and one of the pupils spent a great deal of time with James patiently improving his ability to hit the shuttle. Once the girls were playing competitive games, James would supply them with shuttles as and when needed. The girls were far more disciplined than the boys and at the end of the lesson returned all their raquets to the gym store, but their shuttles were given to James who was sitting on a bench neatly putting them away in the cylindrical tubes especially designed for holding them without damaging their shape.

At break-time some of the older sixth form pupils wandered down to the PE department to look at the fixture sheets for the forthcoming weeks. They all took an instant liking to James.

'Isn't he cute?'

'Who is he Mr Shelby?'

James, for his part, pretended to be coy and shy and hid behind my legs, peering out from time to time to look at the girls!

The morning was a great success and Nicky Brennan, head of the PE department, was so impressed with James' good behaviour and helpfulness that she presented him with a lollipop. James was in seventh heaven!

In the evenings, I allowed James to use my computer, teaching him how to use the Microsoft 'Word' programme so he could type letters to his imaginary friends: Charlie Helpful, Sam and

Chloe. Although James was not yet capable of typing coherent English, he would amass several pages of manuscript which he then printed. He insisted that I read these letters out loud to him and would sit chuckling as I attempted to pronounce the weird sounding 'words' he had created.

He became very adept at making cakes in the 'Cake Factory', a game devised by the Microsoft Company. He knew how to make perfect cakes, but often experimented with wrong designs, because he delighted in the master chef telling him his order was incorrect!

The week passed all too quickly and on the last evening James asked if he could make some flapjacks to take home to his mother. From a very early age, I had allowed James to sit on the work bench in the kitchen and watch me make flapjacks by following the recipe that my mother had left me just before she passed away. By now James knew the recipe by heart and loved his allocated tasks: firstly, the Crunchy Nut Flakes had to be broken into small pieces with a potato masher; then the oats, self-raising flour and Demerara sugar had to be added and mixed in.

James performed these tasks with great gusto, but his favourite part was when the liquid margarine and treacle were added. The resulting mixture was extremely tasty and at this point in the preparation, James would become totally distracted from the main task and fill his little hands full of this sticky substance, rapidly transferring it to his mouth! James was allowed to eat a little, then the remaining amount was spooned into a flat baking tray ready for fifteen minutes cooking in the oven.

Once the flapjack came out of the oven and had cooled sufficiently to be sliced into pieces, James insisted in testing the finished product!

On the Saturday, I drove James back to Ipswich with his two small bags, one containing his clothes and toiletries and one holding his toys and the precious cargo of flapjacks!

Chapter Four: Trip to Dubai

After her visit to Ireland, Jane decided to end her relationship with Richard although he refused to accept or respect this decision and continued to text her and ring her on her mobile every day. He also frequently turned up at her flat and followed her in his car when she was dropping James off at school and picking him up after school. Throughout this period of Richard's dogged pursuit, Jane continued to allow me to see James at weekends and even agreed to go on holiday with James and me in March 2011.

I knew that Jane and I would never be close again. All I hoped for was some form of working relationship so I could keep in contact with James.

I told Jane that I would not consider taking her on holiday with James unless she had completely finished her affair with Richard. She informed me that this was the case and that she had even taken advice from the police over obtaining a court injunction preventing Richard from following and harassing her. Satisfied by these responses, I booked a two week holiday in Dubai at the end of March.

Worried that Richard might follow her and try and prevent her going abroad, Jane left in the early hours of the morning and parked her car at a neighbour's house, arranging for me pick her up from this location. Everything went according to plan and soon we were jetting away from Heathrow Airport to the sunny climate of Dubai.

Unfortunately, from the very first day of our arrival, nothing went well for Jane. The hotel we were staying in was called the Howard Jackson. It was situated not in the tourist area, but near the industrial dockland. The hotel itself was fine, with a spacious bedroom and excellent room service, but being near the industrial area meant there were very few other white, European tourists and the local Arab men would stare at Jane every time she walked down the street, even though she was conservatively dressed. This had a disconcerting effect upon Jane and she felt very uncomfortable.

When I asked her why she was not very cheerful, she asked me if I had noticed the ogling eyes of the local male populace. I admitted that I had seen this, but felt there was nothing that could be done about it. I pointed out that all Arab women walked around in ankle length, black clothes wearing a burka covering most of their face; the sight of a pretty brunette with her face uncovered, must be quite exciting for them! Nonetheless, Jane was unhappy about the situation and berated me for not being more careful about selecting a suitable hotel in a tourist area.

One positive aspect of the hotel was the Jacuzzi and large swimming pool, situated on the flat top of the hotel. Around the hot tub was a large sunbathing area complete with sun loungers and parasols. On most days this area was completely deserted and Jane would stretch herself out in the sun, whilst James and I amused ourselves building ships from empty Coke bottles and then racing them on the swirling, anti-clockwise rotation, of the water in the Jacuzzi.

On one such morning, whilst I was letting the boiling hot sun dry and invigorate my body after a swim with James, I asked Jane why she seemed so disengaged most of the time. Jane's reply came as a huge surprise to me.

'I came on holiday with you, to see if we could be friends again. But I am still very angry with you for telling Richard you loved me and I don't know if I can forgive you!'

She pronounced this statement with such venom that I was shocked and remained speechless for a while. When I finally answered it was with sadness in my voice.

'Jane, if Richard had not threatened me, I would have said nothing, but his continuous verbal rant annoyed me and I wanted to shut him up!'

'Well, you certainly did that and when you told him that you loved me, you destroyed any chance I had of finding happiness with him!'

Jane continued to remain angry and aloof, but James was having a wonderful time.

On enquiring at the reception desk about nearby attractions Jane and I were directed to a local park with cable car rides, dolphin displays, bikes for hire, bouncy castles and trampolines.

James loved the park and soon made friends with other youngsters in the bouncy castle area. His favourite activity though, was bike riding. He would sit alongside me in the specially adapted tricycles and tell me where he wanted me to go. The bikes were relatively easy to peddle which was a good thing because the weather was always extremely hot with temperatures well into the 90 degree Fahrenheit range. We visited all the corners of the park, including the starting point and the control centre for the cable car, a restaurant serving Greek salads, ice creams and cold drinks, and a small lake where paddle boats could be hired. The exercise was good for me and the closeness to James helped me forget Jane's harsh words.

In one of her more friendly moments, Jane suggested that James might enjoy the Dolphin display and so we bought tickets for the 2.00pm show. Before the lights dimmed and the Dolphins swam into view, one of the attendants was selling coloured balls for about a pound each. These were to throw to the Dolphins during the interval. A tannoy system announced that the purchasers of the first three balls retrieved by the Dolphins, would receive a prize.

Jane purchased a blue coloured ball for James which he clutched tightly in his little hands. At the interval, Jane ushered James down to the pool side and at the count of three he threw his ball into the aquarium. The three Dolphins were soon skimming over the water to the area where the balls were floating; the leading two dived under the balls and emerged with one ball each 'glued' to their noses. The third one, much to James' delight, chose his blue ball and sped back to where the trainers were waiting, flipping the ball on to the concrete area where three nets were situated. The trainer picked up James' ball and threw it into one of the nets.

By now James knew his ball was the third one to be chosen and was jumping up and down with excitement. The tannoy system announced the numbers of the first two winners. James waited expectantly, but his little face dropped with disappointment and tears ran down his face when they said the small number of balls being sold meant there would only be two prize winners on this occasion. Jane and I were both very angry and I promised to pursue the matter with the officials once the show was over. James, meanwhile, became more cheerful when I told him that he **would** receive a prize after the show was over.

Despite our vehement protest, the Manager remained unmoved, stating that if James was to receive a prize, the money for it would have to come out of his, the Manager's pocket! This seemed a good solution to us, but not one the Manager was going to opt for! As I could see no point in arguing further, I reluctantly accepted defeat. I settled the issue by asking James to choose any prize from the Dolphinarium Gift Shop. James chose a beautiful porcelain model of three dolphins standing erect on their tail fins which both Jane and I thought was an excellent choice.

On the morning of day five of the holiday, Jane dropped her bombshell! She informed James and me that she had booked a flight home to the UK for herself, leaving at 6.00pm local time. I was dumbstruck! I was aware she was unhappy, but never dreamt that she would take such drastic action!

Over the next few hours I tried my utmost to persuade Jane to change her mind, even offering to repay the cost of her ticket if she would stay. James seemed unconcerned, 'Pookie, don't try and persuade Mummy to stay if she doesn't want to!'

'Look, there you go,' said Jane. 'James will be just fine with you.'

'I am not worried about looking after James. I know he will be alright with me, but it is just not right you flying home early and leaving James and me on our own. After all, I have spent a great deal of money on this holiday, for your benefit as much as my own.' As an afterthought, I added, 'And I may have trouble getting James back into the UK, as he is not my son and I do not have your written permission to travel with him alone.'

'Oh, I'm sure you will bluff your way through!' replied Jane in an offhand manner.

Nothing I said moved Jane at all and she adamantly refused to change her mind. It was a done deal! I did secretly wonder if the texts she had been receiving on her mobile on a daily basis were from Richard and if she had not ended their relationship as promised, but was preparing to meet him back in the UK as soon as possible!

At 4.00pm Jane said her good-byes to James and me. Before she left, she spoke to me out of earshot of James saying, in a softly spoken voice, 'In time, I hope you will be able to forgive me for what I have done.'

And with those final words, she climbed into a red-roofed taxi and headed for the airport.

For the remainder of the holiday, I tried to remain cheerful by filling each day with lots of activities. We spent each morning at the pool side building ever bigger boats and racing them in the Jacuzzi, or swimming across the pool pretending to carry out rescue missions at sea. In the afternoon we visited the local park for bike rides, sessions on the trampoline and bouncy castles and water boat rides.

The location of this last activity was discovered on one of our many bike rides. The boat lake was tucked away in the centre of a flower garden, surrounded by high hedges of yew. Because of its isolation, very few parents found this attraction and James enjoyed the whole lake to himself.

The small boats were powered by two handles connected to paddles, where oars would normally be situated in a traditional rowing boat. James loved powering this boat across the lake, manoeuvring his craft with great dexterity around the small island in the middle of the water. Each session lasted about six minutes, but James would beg me to allow him to go on, again and again, until blisters formed on the delicate skin of the palm of his hands. Even then, he had to be bribed with the promise of a bike ride to leave the boats!

James did not seem to miss his mum and never once talked about her which seemed strange to me. But inwardly I was very pleased as looking after a home-sick youngster, missing his mother, would have been very difficult.

The remainder of the holiday passed very quickly and soon James and I were back in the UK queuing to present ourselves to the lady officer at Passport Control.

I had contacted Jane as soon as we landed at Heathrow. My car was parked in the long-term car park owned by Purple Parking. Jane had arranged to meet James and me in their waiting room, but I inwardly wished that she was waiting outside in the arrival area of Heathrow so that I could summon her if I encountered any problems with bringing her son back into the country.

Our turn to present ourselves and our passports duly arrived. I handed over the documents in my most confident manner and waited patiently for the uniformed lady to scan our passports. She glanced at me and James, checking that we matched our pictures. Then came the dreaded question: 'Is he your son, Mr Shelby?'

I briefly considered telling a lie, after all I felt that James was like a son to me, but common sense prevailed and in a deflated tone I said: 'No, he is not my son.'

'Do you have a letter of permission to take this child on holiday without his parents being present?'

Once again, I had to admit, reluctantly, that I did not have such a letter.

'Then, I will have to call my superior officer.'

In desperation to avoid a huge delay, I explained to the official that James' mother had left us alone, mid-way through a holiday in Dubai! Still not satisfied with my explanation, she reached for the phone. I tried one last throw of the dice.

'He has been on holiday with me and his mother to many different countries in the world, including the USA.'

This last piece of information seemed to do the trick! Fortunately, I knew that the USA had some of the most stringent immigration rules in the world!

'OK!' she said, 'But how do I know this is true?'

I sensed victory: 'Ask James!' I said triumphantly. 'He will tell you where he has been on holiday!'

The lady looked down at James and in a gentle tone of voice said, 'James, where have you been to on holiday?'

James answered quickly and confidently, 'Disney World in USA, Canada, Tenerife and lots of other places!'

The official was visibly impressed but before she finally let us enter the UK she checked both our passports. After leafing through several pages of the two passports and examining the dated stamps from many different countries, she decided that I was not kidnapping James and allowed us back into the country. But before we left she strongly advised me to obtain a letter of permission for future excursions abroad, pointing out that not all immigration officers would be as understanding and lenient as she was!

Chapter Five: Boston West School

After the dramatic experience of the holiday in Dubai, Jane's behaviour seemed more erratic than ever, but I was happy as she was allowing me to see James on a regular basis.

In mid-April I was very surprised when Jane asked me if I would like to look after James, in Boston, for the whole of the Summer Term. In Ipswich, where they were living, Jane had failed to make sure that James was attending school regularly and Social Services had become involved. I never discovered the complete reason for James' poor attendance but knew that one of the main factors was his unhappiness at being bullied at the school by two boys in his class.

Jane had complained to the Headmaster about this but nothing seemed to be done and Jane was very annoyed and unhappy about the situation. She believed that James would be much happier attending one of the quieter Lincolnshire Primary Schools. She also knew that my life was well organised and that I would make sure that James was punctual for school and would attend on a regular basis. Letting James stay in Boston would also give her a chance to *clear her head and enable her to decide what she wanted to do about the Richard situation.*

I could not believe what I was hearing! I was ecstatic, my heart was bursting with joy and I wanted to proclaim the good news out loud to the entire world!

'Yes, of course I would like James to stay with me in Boston and attend a local school. As you know nothing would give me more pleasure.'

'Well, there are conditions,' said Jane.

'OK. What are they?'

'That you get James a place in the Boston West School.'

I immediately knew the reason for this: it was the Primary

School that Jane had attended when she was a youngster living in Boston.

'I'm sure I should be able to organise that,' I replied. 'The school is in the catchment area of my flat. Let me ring the school and arrange an interview with the Headmaster. I haven't worked at the school as a supply teacher, but I do know his name is Mr Schofield and I have met him on a couple of occasions.'

'If you can make the appointment in a few days' time, I would like to be present at the interview to explain why I want James to stay with you and attend this school,' said Jane.

'Before you get too excited,' Jane added, 'this is the only school in Boston that I want James to go to. If he doesn't get a placement there, he will go back to Ipswich with me and attend his former school.'

'No pressure then!' I replied humorously.

So a few days later, Jane, James and I sat in the Headmaster's office and requested a place in the school for James. The Head asked his secretary to join him to take notes of all the important pieces of information.

Jane explained the problems she was having with Richard the ex-boyfriend and the involvement of Ipswich Social Services over James' poor attendance. She informed the Head that James would be happier in a more stable environment. She also mentioned that she was a former pupil of the school. The Head was satisfied with her explanation, but asked if she would be staying with her son in Boston.

'No, not all the time,' replied Jane, 'but I will visit him on a regular basis and if there are any problems Paul can always ring me.'

The Head's main concern was over James' happiness and security. He therefore asked James if he wanted to stay in Boston with me and his little face lit up with pleasure,

'Yes, I would like to stay with Pookie in Boston.'

At the mention of the name 'Pookie' the Head looked quizzically at Jane and me. Jane reacted quickly and explained how James used this family nickname to avoid confusion with his father who was also called Paul.

Then it was my turn to be quizzed, but in a very sympathetic way. Once the Head had ascertained my total involvement with James ever since he was born, he was sure the arrangement would work and asked us James' age. He informed us that there was a place available in the Reception Year but applications had to be made in writing to the Lincolnshire County Council. Once they received the letter, someone in the Education Department would process this application and then write to the school to see if there was a place available. The school had to reply by letter to confirm the availability of a place and in due course the County Council would write to Jane and me and offer James a place. The Head informed us that the entire procedure usually took about three weeks! I was not at all surprised by the length of this bureaucratic process; everything these days was controlled by 'red tape'!

'Is there any way we can shortcut this scenario?' I asked, hopefully, 'because, I am sure that the Ipswich Social Services will be checking on James, which means I will have to try and find a place for him at a local nursery school until one becomes available here.'

The Head was very sympathetic: 'I'll see what I can do. In the meantime my secretary will give you the application form and if you post it tonight that will get the ball rolling.'

Jane and I stood up, shook hands with the Head and proceeded, with James in tow, to the Secretary's Office where we were given a photocopy of the application form. Before we left Jane thoughtfully asked the Secretary about the school uniform and school meals.

Once we left the school, we headed for the Boston outdoor leisure park which was conveniently situated right next to the main Post Office. We decided to travel in separate cars as Jane planned to return to Ipswich once we had filled in the form and had something to eat. James opted to travel in the Red Rocket, even though his mother had a magnificent soft top Audi Quatro sports car!

Once Jane had completed the application form, she addressed

the letter to Lincolnshire County Council Education Department and posted it in the nearby letter box.

Six days later, with some pressure applied by Mr Schofield, James was offered a place at the school with immediate effect. I was delighted. Whilst awaiting the official confirmation, I had been paying for James to attend the Mon-Ami Nursery School and the daily rates were certainly not cheap! I wondered how local working parents could afford to send their sons and daughters to such establishments?

James was looking forward to going to his new school, but he was not the quickest dresser and took an age putting on his socks, smart white shirt, underpants, trousers and red jumper. Finally, after some urgings from me, he was ready for the short walk to the school from the flat.

On the way, we met many other parents escorting their sons and daughters to the school. James was especially pleased to see Emilis, who lived in flat 43, two doors away. Although Emilis was two years older than James, they had played with each other on several occasions and got on well together. I was pleased that James had met someone he knew as this would help him settle in on his first day.

Jane had asked me to ring her when James was starting at the school as she intended to travel to Boston to give him a pleasant surprise at the end of his first day. So at 3.15pm both Jane and I were at the school gates to meet James as he exited the playground.

The form teachers were under strict instructions, from the Head, to supervise their pupils at home time. The children formed an orderly line and were not allowed to pass out of the large, sturdy metal gate until the teachers and pupils had seen a recognisable parent or known responsible adult. As James quietly queued to be dismissed, he saw Jane and me and smiled and waved excitedly. As soon as the teacher let him go he came running over to where Jane and I were standing and jumped into my arms. Then he climbed down and gave his mother a big hug.

James asked his mother if she was staying overnight at my flat. She explained that she had to be back in Ipswich early in the morning, so she would have to travel back tonight. This was a 'white lie'! She planned to stay at a friend's house overnight, as we both had an interview arranged with Boston Social Services the following morning at 10.00.

However, before she left for Nicola's house, we drove into Boston Market Place to purchase some school uniform for James and have something to eat at Pizza Hut.

Chapter Six: Boston Social Services

The following morning, Jane had arranged to meet me in the Market Place at 9.30 so we would both have time to park and then have a quick cup of coffee before meeting Lindsey Bee in the premises of Boston Library.

Jane and I were both sitting on the settee, at the entrance to the Library, when at precisely 10.00am an attractive lady walked down the stairs and introduced herself to both of us. She ushered us into a small room on the ground floor. She was of medium height, with black hair and had the confident manner of someone who had been carrying out this kind of work for a number of years.

Lindsey explained that the interview would be a detailed one and probably take about two hours. Not aware that the report would take so much time, both Jane and I had purchased only one hour parking tickets and told Lindsey that we would need to return to our cars before the expiry time, to purchase further tickets. She had no problem with this and suggested that after an hour of 'grilling' we would probably need a break and suggested a half hour recess at 11.00am.

The interview certainly was detailed and questions were asked about how we met, my involvement with James, Jane's relationship with Richard and all kinds of questions about both of our backgrounds. I was agreeably surprised by some of the statements that Jane made: she told Lindsey Bee of the holidays we had been on together with James and about her absolute trust in me to look after her son. She even volunteered the information that she would trust me to take her son on holiday, anywhere in the world, without her presence. I suppressed a wry smile at the memory of our recent trip to Dubai.

Jane also told Lindsey of the problems she was having with the ex-boyfriend and informed her that James had witnessed domestic violence on more than one occasion. She explained that she was worried that Richard might turn up at James' new school and possibly even try to abduct him so Richard could force her to get back into a relationship with him. She promised to provide Lindsey with a photograph of him for her records.

I was asked if Jane and I had ever been in a relationship.

'No!' I said, 'just very close friends.'

Lindsey's assessment of how long the session would take was totally correct and after two hours of intensive grilling, Jane and I were both exhausted and ready for something to eat before Jane returned to Ipswich.

This joint interview was not the end of the whole process: during the next few weeks, we were both interviewed again, this time separately. Lindsey Bee also visited the Boston West School and had two extensive talks with James; asking him whether he liked his new school or not, how he felt about living with me in Boston, what meals I provided for him, whether he missed his mother, if he understood the role of Paul (his dad) and how he felt about Richard (Jane's ex-boyfriend) and intimate details about bath time and his toilet training. She also called round at the flat to see how James and I interacted with each other; the visit lasted for over two hours, throughout which James was as good as gold!

I felt that the questioning of James and the two hour observation at my apartment was rather intrusive and unnecessary, but as future events were to unfold I was pleased that the final report was so exhaustive in its findings and conclusions!

Chapter Seven: James' stay in Boston

I found life looking after James very demanding as I was still working most days, carrying out supply work as a teacher and had my own busy social life to fit in as well. In order to accommodate my new role as carer, I cut down on my Bridge outings as well as my involvement with the Junior Badminton Team. But in no way did I regret these sacrifices. In fact, I loved looking after Little J! This was a totally new experience for me and I revelled in the challenges it presented!

The other three members of the Boston Bridge team, constantly ribbed me about my role as a *father* at the ripe old age of sixty-five, an age when all of their children had long since 'fled the nest'. But I took their banter in my stride.

I did have to overcome the problem of two commitments: these were my two hour Bridge coaching session on a Monday evening and my two hour Junior Badminton coaching on a Tuesday evening. I was reluctant to cancel my Bridge coaching as I had been paid in advance for this work and felt obliged to complete my allocated ten sessions. With the Badminton there was no financial incentive, merely the satisfaction of training children to a high level of skill and providing them with a lifetime hobby which would hopefully motivate them to keep fit.

The solution to these problems was soon found. Sue, my next door neighbour, suggested I ask Laura, Emilis' Lithuanian mother, to babysit James. Sue felt sure that she would be only too willing to help. When I knocked on the door of number 43, I was greeted by a very attractive lady in her late thirties. Much to my delight, she spoke fluent English and my request was very favourably received. She happily offered to babysit James on both Monday and Tuesday evenings.

I gratefully accepted her offer to look after James for Monday's Bridge sessions but chose to let James decide about Tuesday:

either he could go with me to the Junior Badminton coaching or stay with Laura and Emilis. I felt that James might enjoy attending the Badminton coaching. I was right: James had no hesitation in opting to go with me to the Badminton. Moreover, he was the proud owner of a mini-handled badminton racquet which I had bought him just a few months previously as a birthday present.

James loved being with me at the badminton sessions and spent the two hours sorting through all the tubes of nylon shuttlecocks and supplying each of the four courts with a new shuttle whenever they needed one, or playing quietly with his toys in the large area at the back of the four courts. Sometimes, to the amazement of the twenty or so pupils, he would exercise his little legs by continuously running round the outside of the four courts, often completing ten laps without rest!

After the juniors had all been collected by their parents and the hall was empty, I would spend ten minutes or so training James to hit the shuttlecock over the net. Despite his tender years, James proved an apt pupil and was soon returning a few of my shots.

At the week-ends I would take James and Emilis to 'Play Towers', an indoor play area catering for children of all ages. They would chase each other up the steps, round the various obstacles and down the slides. Although Emilis was two years older than James, James had no problem in keeping up with his friend as they sped around the play park. After half an hour or so they would return to where I was sitting and drink a glass of orange squash and eat some cheese and chips, before resuming their game of chase.

These were blissfully happy times for me. I especially loved meeting James from school at 3.15pm every day. James would emerge from his classroom on the ground floor and stand in line quietly, waiting to be allowed to leave. As soon as his turn came to be dismissed, he would wave to me and then come running over to where I was standing and jump into my arms, his little face beaming with a huge smile.

On one occasion I could not help laughing to myself as I watched James race over to me.

'James, who dressed you after your P.E. lesson?'

'I dressed myself!' said James proudly.

'Well, you have put your trousers on back to front!' I replied, trying not to burst into laughter, 'and you look very funny! You can always tell the front of your trousers by the zip.'

James did not reply but changed the subject.

'Pookie, could you give me a 'piggyback' ride home?'

The distance back to the flat was short enough for me to be able to cope with this exertion.

'OK, hop on!'

I sat on a low stone wall to allow James to climb onto my shoulders and we made our way along the pavement of Arundel Crescent to my flat at the end of the cul-de-sac. Once home, I cooked a meal and then made James complete any homework before allowing him to start to play.

Although James loved his play time, he did not seem to mind doing his homework. He would sit on one of the large leather, comfy chairs and work through whatever assignments were set. James was particularly good at mathematics and whenever the homework included maths, he was in his element. One evening the challenge was to guess a *'chosen'* number by asking a series of questions to narrow down the possibilities until a solution could be found. James proved very apt at this skill although he was not so keen to write down the answers to his work! He usually asked me to complete any paperwork!

Once James had completed any homework set by the form teacher, I allowed him to play. James' play was like no other I had ever experienced. Although his father had bought him models of most planes, James delighted in constructing his own models from pieces of Lego. Once he had constructed several planes, he would load them with cargo and passengers and then transport them to and fro between the various airports. From his extensive travels he knew the names of all the UK's main airports, so the game was very realistic.

Another of his favourite games was 'war battles'. He would divide his planes evenly between himself and me. Once all the weapons of war were ready, we would reconstruct the Battle of Britain. I introduced radar early warning stations and explained to James the role these played in warning the UK air bases of impending German raids. James absorbed all this information and his knowledge and understanding of the world increased day by day.

On one of her week-end visits to Boston to see her son, Jane brought James' new bicycle to my flat. She asked me if I could teach him to ride it. His grandfather had bought the bike for his birthday present. She had spent a short time trying to teach him to ride but said James had no patience and after falling off a few times soon gave up. I promised that I would try to teach him to ride, being secretly confident that I would soon be able to teach James this new skill!

The bike had only two wheels and no supporting stabilisers, so I decided we should start to practise on the boundary of Boston's Cricket Field. This way, if James fell off, he would be landing on grass - much easier on arms and knees than falling onto tarmac!

Teaching James to ride his bike was not difficult. It was even easier than I had anticipated. I started by sitting James on his saddle and explaining to him that if he lent too quickly either to the right or left he would topple over. To illustrate this point, I pushed the cycle quickly to the right and James fell off. With this demonstration firmly implanted in his mind, I told James to sit upright and start peddling. Within a matter of minutes James was cycling! I was having great difficulty in keeping up with his speedy progress and once or twice let go off the saddle so James was actually biking on his own.

'OK, Pookie!' he said. 'Am I ready to go on my own yet?'

'James,' I said breathlessly, 'You have already been cycling on your own for several minutes now!'

James' little face beamed with happiness.

'Have I really?' he said in disbelief.

We spent another ten minutes or so visiting every corner of the field. James was exultant in his new found skill. Then we loaded the bike into the boot of the Red Rocket and returned to the flat. I promised to ring James' mother after tea so he could tell her of his new accomplishment!

Chapter Eight: Fate strikes a cruel blow!

By week six I had completely settled into a steady routine and James and I were getting along famously. Not only had James learned to ride his bike, hit the shuttlecock over the net, play football with considerable gusto and skill, but he was also starting to tell the time and writing out the letters of the alphabet. His form teacher at the Boston West School was very happy with his progress, both academically and socially. Just before the half term holiday, James was invited to the birthday party of one of the girls in his form.

I was still awaiting the final draft of Lindsey Bee's report but she had rung me to say that her department was looking very favourably at deeming me as a Private Foster Carer. However, the final decision would be made by her boss at the Sleaford office. She promised to pop round on Wednesday to see James very briefly and to give me a copy of her report. She asked if a time of 4.00pm would be convenient and I replied that this would be absolutely fine.

After I picked James up from school, we waited in the flat for the arrival of Lindsey. At 3.45pm the phone rang and Lindsey informed me that she was running late with her appointments and that it would be nearer 5.30pm before she would arrive. I decided to take James to the cricket field for some more cycling practice.

We had a really good session of biking. James was now able to get on and off his bike without any assistance from me and could not only cycle in a straight line but also ride in circles as well!

At five o'clock we returned to the flat, stored the bike in the garage and headed up the seven concrete steps to the entrance of the flat. Before I could put the key in to the keyhole and open the door, James asked his fatal question!

'Pookie, what would you do if these steps caught fire?'

I was a little surprised by the question and without a moment of thought replied: 'Well, they wouldn't catch fire because they are made of concrete!'

James was a child with a considerable imagination and not to be deterred by my initial response, he added: 'No, but suppose they did catch fire?'

'Well,' I said, giving the matter a little more thought this time, 'I would climb over the iron railing and lower myself down; then I would tell you to jump into my arms and catch you before you hit the ground!'

'Could you show me?' asked James.

Never, in the whole of my life, has a question had such a fateful and tragic outcome!

I estimated that the distance from the small concrete area at the top of the steps to the forecourt was slightly less than six feet and as I am just over six feet tall this manoeuvre should have been very straightforward.

Taking hold of the mahogany wooden strip on top of the rail with both hands, I prepared to lower myself down. But as I lent backwards and put my weight onto the piece of wood it gave way in my hands and I fell backwards through the air, landing with a resounding thud on the concrete below.

I knew immediately that I was in serious trouble. Everything had happened so quickly that I had been unable to stretch out a hand or leg to break my fall. I had landed with all of my weight onto my left hip. Although I was in no pain, any movement of my legs was physically impossible and I was even incapable of straightening out my left leg which was stretched out at right angles to my body.

James rapidly recovered from his state of shock and came rushing down the steps to where I was lying prostrate on the ground. With tears streaming down his face he implored me to rise.

'Get up Pookie! Get up!'

He even took hold of my hand and tried to pull me to my feet.

'No, James I can't move. You will have to run round to Sue's flat and ask her to ring for an ambulance.'

James rapidly disappeared round the corner.

Before Sue had a chance to arrive a car pulled on to my drive and parked a few feet in front of me. As the driver alighted from her car I recognised the face of Lindsey Bee!

'Oh, have you come to deliver your report?' I enquired, always one to see the bizarre nature of any situation!

'I don't think that is appropriate,' replied Lindsey in her official tone of voice. 'What has happened here?'

'I was showing James how to fly!' I said brightly, trying to remain cheerful in the most dire of circumstances.

Lindsey quickly assessed the situation and taking out her mobile, rang for an ambulance. Meanwhile James appeared with Sue. I asked Sue if she could sort out somewhere for James to stay overnight as it was unlikely that Jane would be able to make the long journey from Ipswich before the next morning. Sue suggested that Laura would be the best option and promised to organise this for me.

The Paramedic arrived and immediately gave me an injection of morphine to deaden any pain I might feel once the state of shock had worn off. He then proceeded to give me a very thorough examination, starting with my toes and working upwards to my legs, spine and neck. He concluded that my neck and spine were OK but my hip was most likely broken.

Five minutes after the completion of the Paramedic's assessment, I heard the unmistakable, strident wailing sound of an approaching ambulance. The Paramedic passed over his notes to the two male ambulance crew members and soon I was being gently lifted onto a stretcher and manoeuvred through the back doors of the ambulance. I managed to wave to James before the doors shut and my last memory was one of a sobbing James standing on the forecourt.

Chapter Nine: Pilgrim Hospital

Once I was lying in a hospital bed and had a chance to reflect on the whole situation, I was furious with myself for being so careless as to not check the security of the wooden railing and totally distraught at the thought of James blaming himself for my accident.

The paramedic's diagnosis proved to be accurate: I had broken my left hip and also my femur. The operation to replace the hip joint and pin the femur took place the day after my admission, but thankfully I was on such high doses of pain killers that I never felt any serious pain!

As I recovered from the anaesthetic, I looked around at the other occupants of the room. They all greeted me and told me their names: Dave, Albert and Hans. I learnt I was in Ward 3A of the aptly named 'Trauma Unit'!

Over the next three days I made an effort to talk to all the other occupants of Ward 3A and came to know a little of their personal lives and the reasons for their admittance to hospital.

Dave was covered in tattoos and I discovered that he was from North Sea Camp, an 'open' prison situated on the coast at Freiston Marsh. Many prisoners were transferred to this prison as they came to the end of their sentences, as it gave them a chance to start to adjust to life outside the prison walls with a little more freedom than in enclosed prisons. The famous politician and author, Jeffrey Archer, had once completed his sentence in this establishment.

Several years previously, I had visited Jane's brother Steven when he was locked away in Rampton Prison, near Doncaster. From that experience I had observed that prisoners were often very reserved. But Dave Cox was different and seemed quite happy to talk about the reasons for his incarceration. He was the owner of a small building firm from the Doncaster area and when the building trade fell on lean times he was offered the chance to make some money by selling imported cigarettes to his family and friends. However, the cigarettes were contraband and no import duty had been paid on them!

When the whole gang were caught, the Judge decided to make an example of the villains and the top operators received lengthy custodial sentences. Dave was low down on the chain, but nonetheless received an eighteen month sentence; very severe, considering the nature of the crime. As he was quick to point out, many burglars and paedophiles are given Community Service Orders for their sentence and yet their crimes are far more damaging to the community than peddling contraband cigarettes!

After he had concluded his fascinating story, I asked him why he was in the Trauma Unit.

'You will never believe it!' he said. 'I was in the gym playing badminton and went for a shot behind me when I tripped over and broke my ankle!'

I was flabbergasted! As a badminton player myself I could totally empathise with this experience and we were soon deep in conversation, reminiscing about our exploits on different badminton courts in Boston and the surrounding area.

In the bed to the left of me was a German called Albert. If Dave's story was fascinating, Albert's was doubly so! He was in for a routine knee replacement. On the day of the operation, he was taken to the Operating Theatre and given a local anaesthetic. After ten minutes or so the surgeons were ready to begin but as a precaution before they started, one of them tapped Albert's knee to see if he could feel anything.

'Yes,' he said, 'it feels like normal!'

The team of doctors were taken aback. With amazement in his voice, one of the surgeons said: 'You shouldn't be able to feel anything at all right now!'

As it was impossible to administer any further dose of anaesthetic they had to postpone the operation for a future occasion. Albert was offered the option of having the surgery done the following day, or returning home and waiting for a new appointment. He decided to return home.

It was whilst waiting to receive his discharge papers that in a very quiet voice he told me of his wartime exploits.

He had been a pilot in the German Luftwaffe, stationed on the coast of Norway. His mission was to fly his reconnaissance aircraft over the North Sea to look out for English boat convoys making their way to the Russian port of Murmansk. Once he had spotted a convoy he would return to his base and radio through its grid reference to the German submarine pens, situated deep in the fjords of Norway's mountainous coastline. The wolf packs of submarines would silently glide out into the deep waters of the North Sea to attack and sink as many of these vital supply ships as they could.

For his services to the German war effort, Albert received a commendation from Herman Goering, Head of the Luftwaffe; this was in the form of a letter congratulating him for his bravery and outstanding flying skill. Albert kept this historic document in his wallet and at my request he showed me the folded letter bearing the unmistakable signature of Herman Goering.

In 1944 Hitler recalled most of the troops and airmen stationed in Norway to Berlin to make a last heroic stand against the advancing Russian and Allied armies. It was in Berlin in 1945 that Albert was captured by the Americans. As a prisoner of war, he was sent to the USA to complete his statutory one year prison sentence and then released to the UK. His flying skills did not go unnoticed by the British government and it was not long before he was flying reconnaissance missions over the USSR for NATO. Whilst living in the UK he married a Lincolnshire lady and was now living on the outskirts of Boston in a small village called Frampton. What a small world this is!

The third member of the ward was a Dutchman called Hans. After introducing himself, he rarely spoke. The few details I garnished about his life came from when he was talking with the nurses or from whispered conversations he had with a lady who visited him. All I learned was that he was a Roman Catholic priest from Holland.

The camaraderie of the occupants in my ward helped lighten

my mood, but what I most looked forward to was the visits of Jane and James. From his first visit, it was obvious that James didn't like the atmosphere of the hospital and hated seeing me lying in the bed not looking at my best. However, his mother had the foresight to bring some paper and crayons and James sat on the hospital floor, near my bed, drawing pictures for me. The stick man in his first picture was lying in a horizontal position and it was easy to work out that this was meant to represent me and my fall from the top of the steps.

'James,' I said in a very gentle tone of voice, 'you must not blame yourself for my accident. I chose to climb over the railing and lower myself down.'

'Yes,' replied James, 'but **I** asked you to do it!'

'Accident are accidents, James. They happen from time to time and no one is to blame. I love you more than anyone on this planet! Come and give me a hug!'

I directed James to the right hand side of his bed to avoid any contact with my replacement left hip and we hugged each other.

'Squeeze me tight, Pookie!'

And I did.

Jane was well aware of the loving bond that existed between myself and James and felt a little guilty about the time when she had forbidden me to see her son. At the end of visiting time she stood at the end of my bed and declared,

'Whatever happens in the future, I will never again try to prevent you from seeing my son!'

I was very happy to hear these words.

For the first day of my lengthy stay in hospital, I was confined to my bed. I was not permitted to climb out of the bed, nor would I have wanted to do so, as moving my left leg was extremely painful. On day two of my recovery, two attractive twenty year old blonde nurses arrived to give me my first physiotherapy session. I noticed that they did not consult the extensive notes held in a metal pocket at the end of my bed; instead they pronounced in a cheerful tone of voice that they had come to get me out of bed and walking! Before they started they stressed the need to get all hip replacement patients walking as soon as possible after their operations.

Any form of movement caused me extreme pain and I did not feel in the right physical condition for attempting to walk for the first time. However, putting such inner feelings aside I started to prepare myself mentally for the effort I knew I would have to make. But before I had time for anything, the sheets were whipped back and the two physios had grabbed my legs and started to swing them across to the left hand side of the bed. I screamed with pain and shouted for them to stop. They reluctantly obeyed and asked me what the problem was.

I was breathless and not in the right mood to give a long explanation of why I did not feel like attempting my first walk, so I quietly asked them to move my legs more slowly. They took not a blind bit of notice of my request and seizing my legs once again started to move them at speed to the side of the bed. By now I was fuming!

'Stop!' I yelled in an authoritative voice.

'What's the problem Mr Shelby?' asked one of the nurses, exasperatedly.

By now, I had made up my mind,

'I'm not going to attempt to do any walking today!' I declared.

The two nurses looked absolutely stunned. They turned to look at each other in a state of utter disbelief at what they had just heard. They turned to face me and glared.

'Have we heard you correctly? You are refusing to do any walking?'

It was my turn to be surprised by their words. Were they not being paid by the state to work for my benefit? Why should they cause me intense pain and discomfort?

Annoyed by their attitude and demeanour I decided to put them in their place, once and for all!

'As far as I am aware, we are still living in a free and democratic country, not in Nazi Germany and I am choosing not to do any walking today!'

They were both stupefied and stood glaring at me for another few minutes before they turned on their heels and left, probably to report me to the Matron for insubordination!

Although I knew that the physiotherapists were only doing their duty, I was not at all happy with their conduct and after giving the matter some serious thought, I decided to mention the incident to the doctors the next morning when they visited the wards for their rounds. All three doctors were astounded to hear of my experience. They asked me if the physios had referred to my notes before attempting to embark upon the walking. I informed them that they had not consulted my records, nor spoken to any of the nurses about my condition.

I was very relieved not to see any sign of these two individuals again! The physios that visited me in the following days were far more considerate and always started by asking how I was feeling and if I wanted to try any walking. I surmised that word of my informal complaint had circulated amongst the Ward Staff and was pleased with the deferential treatment I was now receiving.

On day three, with considerable effort, I managed to climb out of the bed and walk the few metres to the doorway with the aid of a 'Zimmer frame'. However, this small amount of activity totally wore me out and I fell asleep afterwards and did not awaken for over an hour! But by day four I had walked down the full length of the Ward corridor and on day five was taught how to climb and descend stairs, practising on the back stairway which led to the fire exits.

All these walking accomplishments made me feel a lot better. Of my own accord I had stopped taking a lot of the pain killers. I knew that I could manage without Morphine or Paracetamol and therefore restricted myself to doses of Asprin every three hours. Considering the seriousness of my accident I was pleased with the progress I was making and the serious depression which had marked the first three days of my stay was now diminishing.

Being a vegetarian, I was intrigued as to how they would cater for my specialised dietary requirements. For the first three days of my admission I ate very little, but by day four was regaining my appetite and was keen to sample the hospital cuisine. I was delighted to learn that vegetarians and vegans had their own separate menus. I was given a glossy pamphlet crammed full of four pages of delicious sounding meals, including vegetable crumble, sweet potato chips, leak and potato pie and many others. Nor was I disappointed when I first sampled these delicacies; they were every bit as tasty as they looked on the menu!

Chapter Ten: My long road to recovery

Jane and James continued to visit me in the evenings and these were the highlights of my day. On one visit, James brought me some grapes and cheese. By now I was beginning to regain my appetite and cheese was my favourite food! Whilst James ate a box of cheese dunkers I started on my grapes. On a sudden impulse, James asked me if I would like a box of cheese dunkers. When I answered in the affirmative, James reached into his little brown leather school satchel and handed over a new box to me. I became aware that something was amiss by the intensive, expectant look James was giving me. I peeled back the foil which came off surprisingly easily and exposed the empty interior of the container! By now James was chuckling out loud, delighted that his prank has worked so effectively. I found the incident very amusing and was amazed at the thoroughness of James' preparations: he must have spent quite a bit of time getting his 'props' ready.

James quickly passed me one of his own cheese dunkers in case I was disappointed at not having some to eat. What a great little fellow he is I thought, funny and kind; what a marvellous combination! Having completed his trickeries, James asked me if I would be able to attend his Sports Day the next day. I wished I could do this and even considered asking the Matron if I would be allowed out of the hospital for the afternoon and return once the Sports Day was over. But I knew I was not fit enough to undertake this venture. This was the second time in the last two years that I had been unable to attend James' Sports Day, and I was bitterly disappointed, especially after all the running practice James and I had undertaken.

'Unfortunately, little fellow, I will not be fit enough to attend, but remember all the tips I gave you in training!' As an afterthought I added: 'I am sure you will do your best and wherever you finish in your races, I will be proud of you!'

Throughout my interaction with James, Jane seemed very distracted. When James settled himself on the floor to complete some more pictures for me, I asked Jane what was troubling her.

Jane was obviously grappling with a serious issue and with stress showing in her voice, blurted out: 'I am worried that I might get sent to prison for fraud, for claiming Housing Benefit when I was not entitled to it!'

I knew that Jane had continued claiming £500 per month in Housing Benefit, even when Pickle Cottage had been transferred into her name and she was probably not entitled to this money. Each month the cheque was sent to me and I used the money to pay Jane's debts and expenses. But as I was still in the early days of recovery, I found it difficult to concentrate and formulate a carefully considered answer to this problem.

Jane was furious! 'It's just like you to act in a superior manner, as though you are not involved! You too could get sent to prison!'

With this pronouncement, she turned to grab James' hand and declared: 'Come on, we're going and we won't be coming back!'

I was devastated, but I knew how quickly Jane could fly off the handle with little provocation and I knew that she might have second thoughts about the situation once she had cooled down a little. Nonetheless, I did feel guilty for not discussing the matter in more detail, so I rang Jane and offered to have a meeting with her the following morning at 10.00 to try and thrash out a solution.

Fortunately, Jane answered her mobile and had calmed down sufficiently to consider my proposition.

'There are no visiting hours in the morning!' she stated factually.

'No, that's right,' I said, 'but as it's an important business meeting I am sure I can arrange for such a 'one off' visit by speaking with the Matron.'

This proved to be the case and Jane and I were allowed to meet at 10.00am in the waiting room, just past my ward.

'OK!' I said, 'let's get started! What is the current position?'

'I was summoned to a hearing by Tendring District Council to discuss the matter. They showed me photos which they had taken of the four bed-roomed house which Richard and I were renting, with Richard's BMW clearly visible in the foreground.'

'What has this to do with the housing benefit claims?' I asked curiously.

'Well,' replied Jane, 'when I filled out the forms for the tenancy, I stated that Richard was the Landlord and he signed the form accordingly, but as you know this is not true. They have also discovered that I own Pickle Cottage and are now investigating all my claims for housing benefit at this address.'

'Pretty serious, then!' I said.

'When they said they would need to interview my mother, I called a halt to the proceedings and stated that I would need to seek legal advice before continuing. That is where we are at present. They adjourned the enquiry and will re-convene the interview in about three weeks' time. I intend to tell my lawyer that I always considered Pickle Cottage belonged to you because of all the money I owe you.'

I replied: 'For my part, I will support you in whatever way I can even if it means raising money to pay back the housing benefit you may not have been entitled to. You must not feel that you have to face this problem on your own; we will deal with it together. So keep me posted on all developments!'

Chapter Eleven: Setback

During my stay in the Pilgrim Hospital I had many visitors; my bridge colleagues and fellow badminton players all came to spend time with me. Without exception they all wanted to hear how I had broken my hip and femur and I had to recount the story on more than one occasion! By now the other occupants of the ward and many of the nurses knew the story by heart and would joke with me about my efforts to fly!

By the end of day seven, the nurses were thinking about my return home and wanted to know what help would be available to me once I left the hospital. With this in mind I asked my two sisters living in Canada, if either of them would be able to fly to the UK and assist me in my early days of recovery. Both of my sisters were retired so I knew that getting time off work would not be a problem.

Sylvia who lived in Toronto expressed a certain unwillingness to take on the role of carer, as she was uncomfortable about the intimate washing responsibilities this might entail! Delphine, who lived in Victoria, on the West coast of British Columbia, agreed to my request, but stated that she would not be able to travel to the UK for another day or so, as she would have to make alternative arrangements for all her commitments.

I was allowed to leave the hospital on day ten and as it worked out had only one day to cope on my own, because Delphine arrived on day twelve. Although I was almost restored to full health, I still had to endure the indignity and inconvenience of having a catheter fitted. It was very easy to accidently disconnect the tubes and I had more than one mishap at night during my stay in hospital! I was anxious to try and avoid any repeat performances of these accidents now that I had returned home and Delphine would be responsible for changing my bed sheets in the middle of the night and not one of the nurses who were paid to undertake these unpleasant chores.

By this time on my road to full recovery, I could complete most tasks myself but I was warned not to try and tie my shoelaces, nor wash my feet. Moreover, all chairs I sat on had to be a certain height from the ground to avoid dislocating my new hip! When I asked the District Nurse how long I would have to endure these limitations she told me that it would take several weeks for the tissue and muscle to re-grow and in this way secure my replacement hip.

To assist me with the 'forbidden' tasks, a nurse from the local branch of the Outpatient's Care Department came round once a day to help me. She also checked on my general health and asked how I was coping with the catheter. These appointments ceased once Delphine had been in Boston for several days and was capable of taking on this role.

Although at times these restrictions proved slightly irksome they were not overwhelmingly so. On the exercise front, I had been encouraged to walk as much as possible and I endeavoured to comply with this instruction. As soon as Delphine arrived she bought me a retractable walking stick and every day I could be seen covering greater and greater distances around the block where I lived. It was a joy to be home and although I had enjoyed the hospital meals, Delphine was an excellent cook and was only too happy to provide me with my favourite dishes!

The doctors at the Pilgrim Hospital told me that it would be safe to resume driving my car after about six weeks, but I was impatient to be back behind the wheel, especially as I was finding it almost impossible to find an English company that would insure Delphine to drive my car. I found this unbelievable, particularly as Delphine was a UK citizen, had a British driving licence and a twenty-year unblemished record of driving! Even my contacts in the car business failed to surmount this barrier. Therefore, I was keen to overcome the restrictions this placed on our lives by starting to drive again myself!

However, events soon arose which overwhelmed all these concerns about driving, because at the end of the first week, after my discharge from hospital, my health took a turn for the worse.

I was finding it increasingly difficult and painful to pass urine and this started to affect my appetite and sleep. On Friday I was sufficiently ill to ask Delphine to phone the hospital and request a home visit from a doctor.

Red tape and bureaucracy made it impossible to call the hospital directly as calls had to be routed through the National Emergency Help Line. This took an eternity and Delphine ended up repeating the same information to three different people. Finally, her patience and persistence paid off and the hospital promised to send a doctor round to my apartment. He arrived at 2.00pm.

His examination and diagnosis was short and sweet:

'You have a urinary infection, so I will leave you with some antibiotic tablets which you should take three times a day, carrying on until you complete the course.'

With those brief words he left the flat to make further home calls.

I immediately started on my course of antibiotics hoping for some speedy relief from my worsening condition, although I knew full well that it would be at least two days before there was any noticeable improvement.

By the Sunday, further deterioration had set in. By now I was having difficulty eating or drinking and struggled to discharge urine, waking up every half hour during the night.

Delphine made a further call to the National Emergency Help Line and a different doctor was dispatched from the hospital to make a home visit. If I felt the examination by the first doctor had been brief, the second one was even more swift and cursory.

'I'll change your antibiotic tablets,' he stated in a matter-of-fact voice, then left!

I had struggled through the weekend, only semi-conscious for most of the time. Delphine was extremely concerned as I had now become suicidal and threatened to starve myself to death if there was no imminent improvement in my health. Delphine knew me well enough to take this threat seriously and in desperation bundled me into the Red Rocket and despite having no valid insurance drove me to the Pilgrim Hospital's Accident and Emergency Department. On arrival at the hospital's parking lot, she told me to remain in the car whilst she fetched a wheelchair.

Soon I was in the waiting room, sitting in the wheelchair, struggling to remain conscious during the long, three-hour wait before the receptionist told us to go through the door to be examined by one of the doctors.

I remembered little of the following proceedings, but Delphine informed me that a team of four doctors were frantically milling around the bed I was lying on, attaching wires and monitors to my chest and arms. Apparently I was suffering from kidney and liver failure and my heart beat was running at 230 beats per minute! The pads on my chest were ready to receive an electrical jolt to re-start my heart if it failed to respond to the emergency treatment and stopped beating! Various drugs and saline solutions were being administered through intravenous drips attached to my wrist.

It was the magnesium solution that finally started to lower my heartbeat and restore some form of normality to my condition.

Delphine stayed until my bed was wheeled into ward 8A, the heart unit, and then returned to the Red Rocket for the short drive back to my flat promising to return the following day at visiting time.

Chapter Twelve: Final recovery!

I spent a further week in hospital recovering from the debilitating effect of my kidney and liver failure. It took several days before the large number of drugs I was on began to take effect and I started to feel much better. On the fourth day a nurse from the Urinary Unit offered to remove my catheter but she qualified her offer by telling me that if there was any retention of urine the catheter would have to be re-inserted. Nevertheless, I was overjoyed at this news because I knew that the catheter had caused my urine infection and this had led to all the subsequent health problems.

The nurse explained to me what would happen after the catheter was removed: I must drink at least one pint of liquid every hour and my urine must be collected in the specially designed bottles for measurement. After a three hour period, my bladder would be scanned to see if there was any urine retention. If everything was OK the catheter would stay off. I was certain that my bladder would function normally and this proved to be the case: there was no retention of urine and the nurse informed me that the catheter had been finally removed!

Once I was on the road to full recovery, I decided to call Jane from my mobile and tell her about my second spell in hospital. Jane was surprised to hear my news, thinking that I was still at home and getting fitter by the day. Although she expressed her sympathy and wished me a speedy recovery, she did not sound too concerned about how seriously ill I had been. She was busy planning James' sixth birthday at the end of September.

I missed James' visits and was more than willing to talk about him rather than dwell on my own serious health problems. Jane reminded me that not many months previously, I had promised to buy James a trampoline and she wondered if I could afford to buy him one for his birthday. Knowing how much James loved to bounce around on this equipment, I thought this was an excellent idea for his birthday present.

'Yes,' I replied. 'I am very happy to buy him a trampoline provided that I can visit Clacton to see him use it for the first time.'

'Of course!' said Jane, only too happy to comply with this small condition.

During my second spell in hospital Delphine visited me every day but informed me that she would need to return to Canada in about a week's time. This factor made me keen to be discharged as soon as possible. The medication I was on had helped my liver and kidneys to start functioning again and although both organs had not returned to their full working capacity they were well on their way to achieving this. Most importantly of all, my heart beat was now recording a steady 80 beats per minute instead of racing at over 200 beats per minute as it did when I was first admitted.

As I wanted to spend some time with Delphine before she flew back to Canada, I applied a certain amount of verbal pressure on the Matron and was informed that I would be free to return home the following day. My monthly ordeal was finally drawing to a close!

Because I had to wait for my medication to arrive from the Pharmacy and no one could tell me exactly how long this would take, I told Delphine I would ask the hospital to provide transportation for me back to the flat.

So at 2.00pm on day seven, a mini ambulance transported me back to the flat and the two crew members carried all my bags up the flight of stairs and into the front room. They left me to cope with the steps myself, as an important part of my independence relied on my ability to climb the stairway on my own. However, they watched me closely to make sure that I had no problems. As I ascended the seven concrete steps outside the flat, I could not help noticing that someone had placed the mahogany railing (which had caused my fall) onto the small area in front of the door to my flat. It brought back some very painful memories!

Once back in the flat, I felt like a man reborn! Every bodily function was starting to work properly and my appetite was enormous, much to the delight of Delphine who felt that the meals she was so lovingly preparing were finally being fully appreciated!

Chapter Thirteen: A Visit to Clacton-on-Sea

I was keen to see James and Jane as soon as possible and so asked Delphine if she would like to accompany me on a visit to the East coast resort of Clacton-on-Sea. Although Delphine had reservations about Jane's character, she was only too pleased to support me on my first long car trip since breaking my hip.

Jane agreed to meet us with James, but rather than have a pre-arranged time and meeting place she suggested that we give her a call on her mobile when we arrived in Clacton. This turned out to be a good plan as I needed to make several short stops on the journey to stretch my legs and rest my hip. Delphine had packed a few 'nibbles' for the trip and we made our first stop at the Lynford Stag, a well-used picnic area, in the centre of Thetford Woods. Here we had a drink of coffee and ate some fruit and a handful of nuts and raisins.

The journey to Clacton took about half an hour longer than my usual driving time, but at least on arrival I did not feel too tired and my leg and hip were responding well to being kept in the same position for such a long period of time.

As we passed the sign marking the town's limits, Delphine rang Jane to say we had arrived. Jane suggested we meet on the sea front near Angela's beach hut. I knew my way to this venue by heart as James and I had spent many happy hours on the beach near the hut, launching our plastic dinghy into the foaming waves to carry out imaginary sea rescue missions and building fortified settlements of *home-made* cement.

On reaching the area, I parked the Red Rocket in one of the bays especially built for holiday traffic. Within minutes, Jane arrived and had parked her Audi sports car alongside. Almost before her car had made a complete stop, James had the opened the passenger door and was running around the back of the car to greet me. On his handsome little face was a huge smile. Had

I not put my hand out to stop him from jumping into my arms, I may well have been bowled over by James' enthusiasm and exuberance at seeing his best friend standing in front of the Red Rocket rather than lying immobile in a hospital bed!

I decided to sit on the warm bonnet of my car to give myself more stability and then lifted James on to my lap. We hugged each other, before I suggested that we walk over the grass to the path which led to the beach. James raced ahead and I ambled more slowly and sat myself down on one of the sea front benches, thoughtfully provided by the local Parish Council.

I called James over to me.

'I need to tell you something James.'

From past experience, James knew that when I prefaced my sentence by the words, 'I need to tell you something,' what followed next would be very important, so he sat quietly alongside me waiting to hear what I would say.

'I know you did not enjoy visiting me in hospital and that your mother made you come with her. But sometimes in life we do things that we don't enjoy very much for the sake of others. Your visits and the pictures you drew for me kept me going when I was very poorly. If you had not come to see me in hospital, I may not have recovered from my serious injuries. You should be very proud of yourself for what you did. I for my part will never forget how you helped me! To thank you for all your efforts I have bought you a little present.'

With that, I reached into the pocket of my Parka and brought out a small friendship token on a gold chain. This was in the shape of a crescent moon and had a picture of a teddy bear engraved on one side of its flat golden surface, with the word 'Friends' etched above the picture. James was ecstatic with joy and happiness and when I showed him the other half of the charm, identical in all aspects apart from the word 'Forever' being substituted for the word 'Friends' James could barely contain his happiness. I showed him how the two halves of the charm fitted together perfectly to make a full moon. James could restrain himself no longer! He jumped off my knee and went running and skipping over to where his mother was talking to Delphine to show them his new treasure!

Once he had shown his mother the friendship necklace, he came running back to me and jumped into my arms. Fortunately I saw his bounding run and braced myself making sure that my left leg was firmly planted on the ground so that I was not bowled over by his enthusiastic action!

From a distance, I heard Jane shout out, 'Careful James! Remember Pookie's poorly hip!'

I was so brim full of happiness that I felt nothing could harm me – not even James' boisterous enthusiasm! I was confident all the pain and worries of my surgery were now over.

James was keen to talk about his next visit to Boston:

'Pookie, when can I visit Boston to work on the Red Rocket? Tell me how we are going to repair the hole in the door and put in a new dashboard?'

I patiently explained to James how we would repair the hole in the passenger door, but told him that he was in charge of the dashboard. His little face beamed with satisfaction at this new found sense of responsibility.

Our brief visit was soon over and we started on our return trip to Boston. I was delighted that my replacement hip was surviving the pressures of driving very well, but even more delighted that James would soon be visiting me in Boston to repair the Red Rocket!

Chapter Fourteen: Devastating news!

Meanwhile in Boston Delphine had come to the end of her visit. Commitments at home in Victoria were piling up and she desperately needed to get back home to attend to these matters. Moreover, her husband was missing her and was putting pressure on her to return home as soon as possible.

So two days after our trip to Clacton, I drove Delphine to the local bus station where she was to board the National Express to Peterborough. From there she would make her way with a different bus company to Victoria Station in London. Once in the capital city, Heathrow was easily accessible by bus, train or underground.

Delphine and I hugged each other and said an emotional 'good-bye' at the bus station. I thanked her heartily and sincerely for all the help she had given me. I truthfully told her that without her devotion and care I would not have pulled through my terrible ordeal.

I waited for the Peterborough bus to pull into the depot and watched Delphine climb on board before starting the lonely drive back to my flat. As I drove past the bus, I waved to Delphine for one last time.

I had lived on my own for much of my life but over the last four months had been accompanied in my apartment, firstly by James and then by Delphine. Adjusting to the new found solitude proved very challenging. I overcame my loneliness by thinking of my next visit to see James and Jane.

However, at this difficult point in my life I received the following text from Jane on my mobile.

'Paul, leave James and me alone. I am with Richard now and I am pregnant and will marry next year. There is no room in our lives for you. I have always been grateful for all you have done

for my son, but things have changed and you have to leave me alone to get on with my new life and be happy.'

I was devastated. I had suspected that Jane had never really ended her affair with Richard but the news that she was pregnant added a whole new dimension to the situation. When I gave the matter some serious thought, I realised I was not too disappointed about Jane isolating herself from me and wanting to have no further contact, but I was deeply upset by the thought that I would not be able to see James again; after all, it was only ten days ago that Jane had asked me to buy James a trampoline for his sixth birthday and only five days ago she had agreed that James could stay with me in Boston for three weeks during his Summer Holiday!

I decided to ring Jane to discuss the situation especially regarding my contact with James. Jane did not answer the phone, nor did she ring me back when I left her a voice message. In desperation I sent a text to her saying that I was quite happy to leave her alone but I did want to keep in contact with James and also wanted to know what plans she had to repay the £20,000 I had invested in Pickle Cottage! There was no reply! Jane had obviously decided to have no contact with me whatsoever. Frustrated by her behaviour, I wrote to Liz her friend living in Ireland and sent her a copy of the text Jane had sent to me.

In the days of her recovery from addiction to crack cocaine, Jane had been very dependent on the support Liz had given her and she considered Liz to be her best friend and took great notice of any advice Liz gave her. Thus, I felt confident that Liz might be able to change Jane's attitude about my contact with James.

I didn't have to wait many days for some kind of reaction from Jane! A few days after posting my letter to Liz, my mobile 'bleeped' at midnight to inform me that I had received a text message. In my sleepy state I momentarily thought about waiting till the morning to read it then realised that it was most probably from Jane and I would not be able to resume sleep until I had read its content. If the first text I received was upsetting, this one was terrible:

'You are a horrible bastard trying to come between me and Liz; you could not help yourself, could you? You can now spend every penny you have available to try and see my son and I will fight it all the way.'

I was sick to the pit of my stomach; I knew that Jane would be angry with me for writing to Liz but never dreamed for one moment that she would be so spiteful and vengeful. There were only two small positive outcomes from the situation with which I could console myself. Firstly, I had finally managed to get a response from Jane and secondly I had lost nothing by writing to Liz because she could explain my point of view to Jane with regards to my contact with James.

Meanwhile James could not understand what was happening; neither Richard nor Jane ever discussed his friend Pookie and if he mentioned his name he was told in no uncertain terms to 'Shut up!' He could not understand why Pookie never came to visit him and in the bleak months James often held his friendship charm in his right hand and thought back to the day at the sea front and the words which Pookie had spoken to him. Whenever he recalled this experience a sadness enveloped him and tears ran down his cheeks; he could not understand why Pookie no longer wanted to visit him. Perhaps the amulet had magical properties and if he rubbed it hard enough and made a wish, Pookie would appear? He tried this on many occasions without success. Pookie had disappeared completely from his life. He began to wonder if he had done something wrong, something which had so upset Pookie that he no longer wanted to see him. Perhaps Pookie was annoyed with him because he had caused him to break his hip; he felt so guilty and this made him very sad.

One day when he persisted with his question about Pookie, despite the fear of a verbal lashing, his mother casually answered: 'Oh, I suppose he is too busy with his life in Boston to drive down and see you.'

James was bitterly disappointed and greatly missed his best friend but there was nothing he could do; he was utterly powerless and helpless!

Chapter Fifteen: Final Contact!

After several months of legal procedures I was allowed to see James briefly at the Cafcass Office in Colchester. This visit was magical: at about ten minutes past four, I heard Sally giving directions to Jane on her mobile phone, as to the whereabouts of the Cafcass Centre. She mentioned Head Gate and I knew they were very close. The tension was unbearable, I was struggling to contain my urge to race out of the room and greet James at the main entrance. Fortunately, it was only a few minutes later that the door to the contact room opened and James appeared with the Guardian.

He raced over to where I was sitting;

'Pookie! Pookie! Pookie!' he cried out with enormous excitement in his voice and immediately jumped onto my knee and gave me a big hug.

Any fears that I had harboured about James reacting in a hesitant and reserved way immediately vanished in a wave of uncontrolled, raw emotion. Had Sally Hacknell not suggested that James must be hot and offered to take his coat, James and I may have hugged each other for considerably longer than we did! Sally made her excuses, stating that she needed to talk to Jane and left the room.

The unbreakable bond of friendship which had always existed between James and I was renewed and the fifty minutes of contact time passed like a blur of lightning. I asked James about his new school and the subjects he was studying. James carefully and meticulously explained to me the sums he was doing.

'They give us a number, say 20 and another number like 15 and we have to work out how they match.'

'And what is the answer?' I asked, curiously.

James' reply was instantaneous: 'The number is 5.'

I tested James on several other numbers and his answers were correct every time!

'You must be one of the best at maths in your class!' I commented.

'Well, I am in the top group, but there is one other boy better than me.'

'I'm sure you'll catch up with him in no time at all!'

I then asked James if he would like to open his Christmas and Birthday presents and James became very animated. He carefully opened each present in turn and examined them in great detail. He loved the Wall-E robots and all of the books I had carefully chosen for him, especially the car encyclopaedia.

I asked James if he remembered the song from the *Italian Job*. With a little prompting at the start, James quickly burst into voice:

'This is the self pres..er..vation so..ci..ety!'

We both sang this refrain, with great gusto, several times.

We reminisced about the Walt Disney film called 'Up' and James talked about Kevin, the rare bird that the explorer had tried to capture.

I was surprised that James had not once mentioned his new baby brother, so I asked him what his name was.

'Joshua Henson Gray-Steel... and that's a long name!'

Apart from answering my question, James volunteered no further information about the baby.

At five o'clock, all too soon, the door opened and Sally returned to the room. She asked James how he had got on and in response to her question I asked him sing the refrain from the Italian Job. James burst into voice, singing this several times before telling Sally about his favourite parts of the film: the Mini car chase and the bus with the gold bars, perched on the edge of the cliff. He asked me if I could get him a DVD of the film and I promised to try.

Sally informed James that it was time for me to leave. James turned imploringly to me. 'Do you have to leave? Why can't you stay?'

When Sally reiterated that I had to leave, James dashed over to where I was sitting and, once again, jumped onto my knees.

He clung to me, hugging and kissing me at the same time.

Up to this point in time I had remained calm and in control of my emotions, but now, faced with the possibility that it might be many months, or even years, before I would see him again, I became tearful. In order not to release my own deep emotions I tried to distract James and myself by introducing a new topic.

'Guess what car I have now?' I asked.

'I don't know.'

'I've still got the 'Red Rocket!'

James was really excited by this piece of news, but I also detected a trace of sadness in his demeanour.

'It still has the hole in the passenger door, and I'm waiting for you to help me fix it and to rip out the old dashboard and put in a new one!'

James' little face showed his worst fears, 'Mummy told me that I can't go to Boston ever again and Richard told me that you have caused Mummy a lot of trouble and this is a 'one off' visit.'

'Well,' I said, 'Do you want to see me again?'

'Yes! Yes! Yes!'

'Then the only thing we can do is to try and change Mummy's mind,' I stated, trying to display more confidence than I really felt.

I reluctantly rose and slowly headed towards the door.

Author's footnote:

I have not seen James since this visit but every single day I put on my friendship necklace and this reminds me of the happy times James and I spent together. I also continue to be the proud owner of the 'Red Rocket' which has now clocked up an impressive 300,000 miles; it still needs the dashboard replacing and the hole in the passenger door repairing. I eagerly await James' visit to Boston to carry out these tasks!

Lightning Source UK Ltd.
Milton Keynes UK
UKOW06f0959160715

255250UK00001B/34/P